THE BIG RIVER

PETER CUMYN

Pitullie Publishers

Pitullie Publishers

The Big River
Copyright © 2022 by Peter Cumyn.

ISBN 978-1-7780009-0-4 (paperback)
ISBN 978-1-7780009-1-1 (ebook)

Interior design by Aaxel Author Services
Cover design and illustrations by Paul Abraham

This is a work of fiction. Names, characters, events and incidents are the products of the author's imagination. Any resemblance to actual persons, living or dead, or actual events is purely coincidental.

To my wife Madeleine,
our children and grandchildren.

Mid-October 1992

Gerald Symons takes down his gun and puts a handful of cartridges into the pocket of his shooting jacket. He steps out of the mudroom of Ardeath House and quietly shuts the heavy green door behind him. He remains still for a while, lost in thought, his eyes blinking in the sunlight. It is a mild afternoon, typical of this season in Scotland, and the skies show blue and grey through the golden leaves and twisted branches of the beech and sycamore trees.

His spaniel Topper hears him and starts to jump against the enclosure of the kennel, whining and barking in excitement. Topper sees that his master has his gun nestled in the crook of his right arm. He hopes that they will take a walk beyond the grounds of the house and shoot a pheasant or two.

Gerald goes to the kennel and releases the dog. Together they set out under the trees, Topper darting off with his nose to the ground looking for scent, Gerald setting his course towards a breach in the high brick wall which envelopes the house, isolating it from the farms and bits of woodland that lie beyond.

Five minutes later, they pass through the breach in the wall and Gerald loads his gun. They start hunting along the gorse bushes and brambles lying beyond.

All is still, as if suspended in time. Only small insects are moving, making a faint buzzing noise as they revolve in the air, appearing and disappearing in endless patterns. Individually, they would seem too small to be significant, but collectively, their presence is as palpable as that of the man and his dog.

Suddenly, the silence is shattered by a single shot from a gun. There is an unusually harsh and strident quality to the sound, and in the wake of its echo come other noises, a moan, a falling body, gushing blood.

In a treetop down towards the end of the wall, some hoodie crows start from their stillness and hasten off to another place.

The yellow gorse flowers at the foot of the wall still give off their strong fragrance, and the small insects continue to fly their patterns in the air. However, there in the shadow of the wall, Gerald Symons lies dead in a growing pool of blood, his face brutally blackened and disfigured and his gun lying beside him.

2

August 2021

Jill walked down Union Street in central Aberdeen on her way to the bank. It was a warm day and the rose bushes which bordered the sidewalk gave off a delicate perfume.

Jill was now just under forty years old. She had a finely sculpted face with high cheekbones and mid-length honey-coloured hair, which she had tied up that morning in a ponytail. She also had a wonderfully trim, energetic body.

She had a lot on her mind but kept saying to herself, "Hold your horses, Jill. One thing at a time. Let's get that cheque deposited first." Then she could turn her attention to the rest.

It was an important cheque for her. A nice amount, yes, but more than that, it was payment for an article that had caused a fair sensation when it was published in the papers two weeks before. She had even been interviewed on television.

Jill had written other articles before, but this one was clearly her best. It was the story of three boys and how their young lives had been impacted by the fact that their fathers had been sent to prison: one for pushing drugs, one for fraud, and one for violent assault.

The interviews of the boys had required a lot of patience and a lot of tact, but Jill was good at that. She was someone people felt that they could confide in, that they could trust.

Just as she was about to go across the street to the bank, a rough voice came from behind her. "Hey you!"

Jill knew instinctively that the voice was directed at her. It had to be; there was no one else nearby. The voice was menacing, even violent. The kind of voice that spelled trouble. A slight feeling of nausea, of fear, welled up inside her. She hated that feeling; it had its antecedents, ones that she preferred not to remember. "Control that fear, Jill," she said to herself, turning around. "Don't let it show."

The man was big and wore a black T-shirt. His arms were muscular and covered in tattoos. His head was shaved, and the skin of his face was blemished and bore at least one scar. "Yes, you," he said, his half-closed eyes driving into hers. "You're Jill Brown, aren't you? And you wrote that article."

Jill forced herself to answer. "Yes, I'm Jill Brown. Who are you?"

"Callum's father." Callum was the eighteen-year-old boy whose father had gone to prison for assault. Presumably, the father was now out on parole. "What business have you to write about me and Callum?"

Jill simply shrugged. "That's my business. I write articles."

The man's face hardened. "I'll teach you some manners," he said. He took a step towards her.

She could now smell his breath. It was stale and nauseating. She stood her ground, but it wasn't easy. "I like your son. He seems very mature. He has told me about his girlfriend, about how he wants to go into the merchant marine. Perhaps he misses you as well. When did you last see him?" The man hesitated. "Have you been out for long?" she asked.

The awful thought occurred to Jill that maybe the man had escaped from prison and was on the run. This could make it a very tricky situation. She tried to remember some of the techniques she had practised a few years past when she taught gymnastics and basic martial arts at the police academy in

Glasgow. She fervently hoped it wouldn't come to that; she was definitely out of training. She must correct that. "Relax, Jill," she told herself. "Take a deep breath."

"I'm out on parole," said the man.

"Have you gone to see Callum? I think he would like that."

"Why?"

"You're his dad. A son needs a father, even if everything is not perfect between them."

"You don't know his mother. I don't want to see her again."

"But she's not Callum. I think he would like to see you. And you should know that he was very happy that I was writing about him. It made him feel important."

Jill was beginning to feel that events were coming back within her control. Something like a conversation was taking place. The man stood there silent for quite a while, and the tension between them began to ebb away. Suddenly, he turned and, without a further word, walked off down the street.

Ten minutes later, Jill was sitting alone in a cafe staring at a glass of cold white wine; it was medicinal, she thought to herself. If this was how folks were like up here in the north-east, she would be better off returning to Glasgow! "No," she said to herself. "I'm only joking." And in any event, there was Sylvia.

Sylvia and Jill had met by chance two months previously. Jill had by then left her job at the police academy and turned to her second love, women's clothes. She was in charge of sales in a dress shop specialising in affordable fashion on Glasgow's premier shopping street, Sauchiehall.

That day, a customer came in and after a few minutes asked if she could try on a summer dress. It was Sylvia, down in Glasgow for a short holiday. In the dressing room, as Sylvia was adjusting the dress at her waist, Jill reached out to correct a wrinkle on the back and her hand lightly grazed Sylvia's bare shoulder. Their eyes met in the mirror, and it was as if an electric shock had passed between them.

"You look stunning in that dress," Jill said, but she then felt slightly embarrassed. "I mean," she added, correcting herself, "it really suits you."

"That's nice of you," answered Sylvia, smiling at Jill's awkwardness. "I like it as well. I think I'll take it."

Later, when Sylvia was at the cash register paying for the dress, she asked Jill her name. "Do you ever come up to the north-east?" she asked. "If you do, let me know. I would love to show you a bit of our countryside." She took a bit of paper out of her purse, wrote down her email address, and gave it to Jill.

All that afternoon, Jill just couldn't get Sylvia out of her mind. There was something special and yet vulnerable about Sylvia, something that Jill wanted to know more about, to get closer to. That same evening, she decided to take up Sylvia's invitation and she sent her an email.

Two weeks later, she visited Sylvia for the weekend and the two got along really well together, so much so that Jill stayed on for an extra two days. They enjoyed the same things, thought many of the same thoughts. Their time together showed them just how lonely they each were.

When Jill finally left to return to Glasgow, Sylvia was nearly in tears and asked Jill to come back, adding that she could stay for as long as she wished. They embraced, and Jill promised to call Sylvia each night after work.

That was three weeks ago.

Jill realised that she had been sitting at that table for at least ten minutes without even tasting her wine. "Right! The cheque's deposited," she said to herself. "But what do I do next?"

She had been sleeping on the sofa in Sylvia's living room for the last three days. She was happier than she had been for a long time and the arrangement seemed to suit Sylvia as well. However, it was all very temporary, and some more permanent decisions were required. For example, Jill had been offered a part-time job at the local Post Office. This would be perfect, as it would permit her to continue writing articles. Should she accept the job before someone else did?

The real issue was her relationship with Sylvia. Until now, they had both held back from revealing their innermost thoughts to each other. Jill really liked Sylvia and could feel a strong emotion growing within her. She also felt physically excited by her. Never before had she felt this way about another woman. Men, yes, but women, no. If she was to move in with Sylvia, the relationship between them would almost certainly change dramatically. This would represent an enormous step for her and involve a big change in her life.

Jill had few ties to Glasgow: no family, no close friends. She now realised that she had become bored by her job in the shop and yearned for something new, and possibly also for someone new. Sylvia seemed to be becoming that someone. "Well, Jill," she said out loud. "To hell with convention. Go for it!" She didn't touch the wine, left a bit of money on the table, and headed for her car.

3

On that same morning, Sylvia went to visit her ailing mother in Old Aberdeen. She parked out in the street, rang the front doorbell, and without waiting for a response, went inside and entered the sitting room where Mary Cowan, her mother, generally passed the greater part of her day.

Sylvia was tall and slim, with dark hair cut rather short so as to frame her face, which was long and graceful. She was single, and in her late forties. Her brown eyes shone with a soft warmth and her mouth was full and smiled easily. She was modest and unassuming; perhaps excessively so. She was wearing a pale mauve cotton blouse with short sleeves and dark blue slacks that fitted her easily and made her look both very comfortable and very attractive.

"Hello, Mum," she said, giving her mother a kiss and sitting down in an armchair next to her. "How are you making out?"

"Fine thanks, dear. You look very smart. Is that blouse new?"

Sylvia laughed. "Come on, Mum. I've had it for years!"

Mary frowned. "I don't remember seeing it before. Are you going somewhere special?"

That morning, Sylvia had wanted to look her best because

of Jill, but she could hardly tell her mother that. "No. Nowhere special. What are you reading?"

"Just the papers. Do you still have your friend visiting you?" Mary was still looking at her daughter's blouse.

"Yes. It's really nice having her, particularly now that I'm working from home. We go for long walks and give each other cooking lessons!"

Mary held her newspaper up. "Syl. There's an article here that I would like to cut out. Perhaps we could send it to John."

"John?" Sylvia took a deep breath. These conversations with her mother always came back to the same subject: John, her oldest brother, the brother who had emigrated to Canada almost thirty years previously.

"Yes," said her mother. "The article is about sheep, and reminds me of our farming days at Bonnycastle, when John was still at home."

Sylvia laughed scornfully. "I imagine that Bonnycastle and the sheep are a long distance from John's mind just now."

Mary chose not to be distracted by her daughter's outburst. "Your father handled the cattle and the crops, and I took care of the sheep. I remember those long cold winter nights when I had to sit out in the byres waiting for an ewe to give birth. It could take an eternity. However, John was more involved with the shearing than with the lambing."

Sylvia sighed. "Bonnycastle, the sheep, John. Mum, perhaps it would do you good to think about something else."

Mary still took no notice. "Do you remember how you all used to help me with the shearing? You and Duncan would manage the gates, and John would grab each ewe as her turn came and throw her on her backside while I did the shearing. At the end, John was pretty good at doing it all by himself."

Sylvia was finding these conversations with her mother more and more difficult. It was not that she hadn't liked her oldest brother - quite the contrary. She had worshipped him when she was younger and he was still at home. He was truly her big brother. It was simply that Sylvia was not one for reminiscences, and her mother did tend to go on and on about the same things. "We haven't heard from him for a while," she said thoughtfully. "When was his last letter?"

Mary shrugged. "His last letter? I suppose three months ago. He isn't the best when it comes to writing letters."

"It's too bad," Sylvia said. "You would have thought that he could do more than just send us his occasional news. It doesn't seem right to me."

"I totally agree," Mary said, "and I keep asking him to come home for a visit, but he never gives me a satisfactory reply.

"He's always been like that. It makes me quite angry. What bothers him so much? Why shouldn't he come back for a visit?" Sylvia was getting worked up. "It's as though we weren't important to him. You in particular, his own mother!"

"It wouldn't be easy, I suppose," Mary said. "Not living where he lives, way up in northern Canada. Just getting to an international airport would be a major undertaking." She paused and looked sadly down at her hands. "You know, Syl, I think that if he doesn't come back to see us soon, I may never see him again."

Sylvia thought of protesting, but her mother was quite right.

"Worse still, it may be my fault. It's a thought that has always troubled me."

"Your fault? How can you really feel that, Mum?" Sylvia asked.

"Well, when John left for Canada, there was a possibility that it was somehow connected to Gerald Symons' death."

"Yes, you've said that before."

"You were still pretty young at the time. But there was talk. A lot of talk. And John left only two or three weeks after the accident. If it was an accident."

"Don't you think that it was an accident?" Sylvia asked.

"Yes, I suppose I do. I certainly don't think that John murdered Gerald. But there was bad blood between them because of Gerald's terminating our tenancy and because of Jessica. That's why there were rumours, I imagine."

"But there's still no need for you to blame yourself for John's staying put in Canada."

"Not so, Syl. I failed John. As a mother, I should have known in my own mind that he had absolutely nothing to do with what happened to Gerald. I should have made that clear, not only to him, but also to everybody else. But I didn't." Tears welled from Mary's eyes, and she reached for a handkerchief and blew her nose. "Who could blame John if he felt a bit let down by me in those circumstances? How I would like to see him again!"

Sylvia waited until her mother had recovered. "Mum," she said. "You shouldn't run yourself down like that. John probably had all sorts of reasons for leaving, ones that had nothing to do with Gerald Symons' death. Who knows? Anyways, whatever his reasons were, it's still not right that he never comes back to see us."

Sylvia thought that she might then change the subject. "Has Duncan been to see you?" she asked of her other brother. And not her favourite one.

"Yes, he came yesterday," Mary replied. "He's having difficulties with his job at the bank."

"What kind of difficulties?" Sylvia asked. "I seem to recall he was thinking of quitting." The trouble with Duncan, she felt, was that he was always quitting. First, he quit the army. Then he quit his marriage. Now, it seemed it would be his job at the bank. "No," she said to herself. "I'm being too hard on him."

Mary continued talking on about Duncan and the bank. "You know, Syl," she concluded. "I have five grandchildren. Five! And do I ever see them? No! John's two I have never even met. Total strangers! My own grandchildren! And Duncan's three have now moved down south with their mother. I'll probably lose sight of them as well. It's awful." She thought of adding a comment about the absence of children on Sylvia's part, but wisely refrained.

"I'm not getting any younger, either. I wish I could see John again. I've asked him time and again to come and visit us, but never with any success."

Sylvia glanced at her watch. Jill would be heading back to Ardeath by now. She imagined how they might greet each other this time. A big warm hug. Hmmm. It was great having Jill around; she gave Sylvia a new energy, a new reason to admire the countryside around her, a new desire to discuss things and to reflect on them. Jill was beginning to occupy a big space in her thoughts and in her life.

Sylvia looked at her mother sitting in the faded velvet armchair by the window. Mary looked old. "Mum," she said rapidly. "I have an idea. Why don't we get Duncan to go out to Canada to find John and convince him to come home for a visit? What do you think? Duncan might be able to persuade him."

Mary looked up. "Do you know? That's not a bad idea. If Duncan actually went there, John might find it more difficult to refuse. A trip like that would also do Duncan a world of good."

"You speak to him, Mum, will you? You have more influence with him than I have." Sylvia didn't want to talk to Duncan herself.

"But would Duncan agree to make such a trip?" Mary asked. "To Labrador? Just to speak to John?"

"I think so, especially if we convinced Duncan that in doing so, he would have a good chance of success." Sylvia rose and started heading for the door. "Where is it that John lives? The town with the funny name."

"Makkovik," said Mary. "He lives near Makkovik. On a river called the Big River."

4

Sylvia and Jill set out for a walk along the narrow road leading past the cottage where Sylvia lived. It more resembled a country lane than a proper road. It had been paved a long time ago and seemed to have sunk into the ground over the years.

Crowding in on each side were roughly trimmed hedges of beech and hawthorn. Beyond the hedge on their left was a large field where the barley had recently been harvested and large round bales of straw lay scattered on the golden stubble.

"I needed this walk badly," Jill said. "I've had a rough morning." She was still shaken by her encounter with the man with the tattoos.

"Well, I had two great ideas this morning," Sylvia said, putting her arm around Jill's shoulder as they walked along together, side by side.

"What are they?"

"The first is that you should stay here with me, for good. Will you?" She gave Jill's shoulder a little tug.

Jill laughed and gave Sylvia a quick kiss on the cheek. "I'm thinking about it, Syl. I really am. What was the second idea?"

"Oh, come on," Sylvia teased. "Do you think that I'm

going to let you off that lightly?"

"We can always return to your first idea later."

"Mmm. Well anyway, my second idea was to persuade Mum to ask my brother Duncan to go out to Canada and get John to come back for a visit. She's been pining to see John again."

"Sounds like a good idea," said Jill. "You've never told me much about your brother John. When did you last see him?"

"We haven't seen him for almost thirty years. He has never returned to Scotland since he left. Not once."

"That's strange. Why not?"

"Oh, for a variety of reasons, I suppose. But I really miss him. He and I were very close when we were growing up together. He left for Canada quite suddenly. I was about twenty at the time and it left a big hole in my life." Sylvia fell silent as she thought back to those days.

"Were you still living out here on the estate when he left?" Jill asked.

"No, we had moved by then. My father died when I was sixteen and John became the head of the family, together with Mum, of course. Dad died of drink - I never told you that. At the end, he made life difficult for Mum, and really, for all of us, and the farm started to go downhill. After he died, Mum carried on with the farm and we all pitched in, but it wasn't enough, and our landlord terminated the tenancy and kicked us off the land."

"That must have been a terrible shock!"

"And how! But there was nothing that we could do. Mum was more or less resigned to the situation, but John was furious. He even talked of going to see a lawyer."

"Is that when he emigrated to Canada?"

"No. That happened later."

They continued on their way and at the end of the stubble field came to the start of a high brick wall. To their left was the entrance to a dirt road leading up a short hill between two green fields in which were grazing a number of fat black Angus cattle. At the top stood a stone farmhouse and a number of farm buildings. A sign at the spot where they now stood said Bonnycastle.

"That's it," said Sylvia, pointing up the hill. "Our old farm. Bonnycastle. It brings back memories."

"Do you think that John wanted to continue farming here?" asked Jill, picking up the thread of their former conversation and looking up the hill. "And then the tenancy was terminated. Is that why John eventually left Scotland?"

"I don't think he wanted to farm. He was always very good at his studies. Definitely the brightest of the three of us. He even went on to study botany at the University of Aberdeen. No. I don't think he would have wished to take up farming after that."

"So, after university, he was faced with the decision of what to do next?" Jill, being herself faced with the decision of what to do next, was very interested in the reply.

"I guess so. He had several options and I suppose emigrating to the New World was one of them." They came to a bad patch in the road and Sylvia had to leap over a series of potholes.

"You don't sound convinced."

"I'm not. To Labrador? Why choose to go to Labrador?"

"For the sake of adventure. To make a change. Much more interesting than continuing to live in the same way as before, in the same setting." Jill was thinking of her own life at this point.

They walked on together. A large cock pheasant was sitting on top of the wall not far from them. With a raucous screech, he took flight and glided across the road into the barley stubble for his afternoon forage.

"There was something else that happened just before John left," Sylvia said.

"What was that?" Jill was curious.

"Gerald Symons' death. Gerald was our landlord, and father of the present owner, Keith Symons. Do you see that spot in the field where the wall has collapsed? That's where they found the body."

"Found the body?" Jill asked. "Do you mean to say that he was murdered?"

Sylvia shook her head. "No. Not quite. Apparently, it was an accident. It happened just over there. Come and I'll show you."

They went through a gate and walked up the field along the side of a high wall. On the further side of the wall were tall trees, and at the foot of the wall on their side were brambles and thorny bushes of gorse, bristling with yellow flowers. Sylvia stopped at a certain point. "It was here. There's nothing much to see now."

"No. Of course not. Tell me. What happened exactly?" Jill's instincts as an investigative journalist were coming to the fore.

"Gerald often came along this side of the wall to shoot pheasant. We sometimes saw him or heard his shots from our house up on the hill."

"Where did he live? In Ardeath House, presumably."

"Yes. The big house is nearby, just beyond the wall. He would bring his spaniel, and the dog would go under all these brambles and gorse bushes and flush out the pheasants, making for an easy shot. Bang! One more for the freezer. Or the game merchant."

"Was Gerald alone? How did he die? What killed him?"

"None of us saw anything, but we heard later that he was alone, and that he died from a blast from his own gun. Point blank. In the face. It couldn't have been a pretty sight."

"Was the gun in any way damaged? Had one of the barrels burst?"

Sylvia wondered why Jill wanted to know so much about Gerald Symons' death, but continued nonetheless. "I don't think so. If I remember correctly, they found his gun on the ground beside him, off safety. In one barrel, the cartridge was spent."

"What time of day was it?"

"Just after lunch."

"How soon after the accident was it that they found the body?"

"Perhaps two hours later. Keith came across it. His mother Andrea was with him. They went back to the house and called the police. There was an investigation and the police concluded that it had been an accident. It was plausible enough. Gerald could have been about to shoot and could have taken the gun off safety. He could then have stumbled and fallen, and his gun could have discharged."

Jill remained silent for a long while, looking in one direction and then in the other. "Gerald was alone. There were no witnesses. And so the police concluded that it was an accident." She was intrigued. There was certainly something here that was worth pursuing.

The two returned to the road and continued along beside another section of the wall. "Why would John have had anything to do with Gerald's death?" Jill asked.

Sylvia shook her head. "It's complicated. You see, John and Gerald's daughter Jessica were deeply in love with each other. They had been going together for quite a few years and Gerald didn't approve. One day, he and John even had a fight. On the day of Gerald's death, John was out here seeing Jessica."

"But surely you don't think that John did it? That he murdered Gerald?"

"Absolutely not. John would never have done anything like that."

"So why did he leave Scotland? Why leave and never return?"

"Well, some fingers were pointed at him. Mum was

saying to me just this morning that she herself may have had her doubts, that she bitterly regretted not having backed John to the hilt. That may have had something to do with John's decision."

They continued on in silence. Sylvia walked steadily, holding her body very erect. Jill's pace was more energetic, her body more supple, and occasionally she had to slow down so as not to pull ahead.

"And what about John's love affair with Jessica?" Jill asked.

"It ended. I sometimes wonder if that wasn't also a reason for John's leaving. Perhaps he wanted to break off their relationship and couldn't think of any other way to do so."

"And what about you, Syl?" Jill asked, looking at her with a sly smile. "Have you had a few torrid love affairs of your own? Have there been many men in your life?" It was a question she had been wanting to ask for a while.

Sylvia hesitated. She wasn't used to being open about her private life. Not even with herself. "I've nothing against men, really. And yes, I have had the occasional affair with a man. To tell you the truth, also with a woman." She made a face. "Jill. To be frank, my love life has never been a great success. I could tell you all there is to know in five minutes. I've never been able to find the right person." She laughed bitterly. "Perhaps my hormones are deficient, but I don't think it's that. Just the luck of the draw, I guess."

"And you," she turned to Jill, "have you had many men in your life?"

"Yes, I suppose you could say so, but I've never had a relationship last for more than a year or two."

"Why do you think that's so?" Sylvia asked. She was interested in what Jill would say.

"Like you, perhaps I never met the right person," Jill replied. "I never found someone who wanted to treat me on equal terms. I always felt that somehow, I was being used."

"But still, did you enjoy it?" Sylvia asked. "Did it give you pleasure when you were in bed with a man?"

"Oh, for sure, most of the time," Jill said.

"Me no," Sylvia said, "but I think that it must have simply been because I didn't love the man I was with."

They walked on in thoughtful silence, and the cottage came into sight. Jill started to tell Sylvia about her encounter with the man with the tattoos. "I was pretty scared, I can tell you. He was very big."

"Couldn't you just go quickly into the bank, or a shop?"

"I didn't have the chance. He was right there behind me." Jill made a face. "I could even smell him." What Jill really hadn't liked was that sensation of fear that had invaded her when the man first spoke to her. She needed to exercise more self-control than that.

"I can't for the life of me understand why people have tattoos," Sylvia said after a short while.

Jill laughed. "I have one."

"No! Jill? Really? Where is it? Is it a picture or just words?" Sylvia was incredulous. "Show me."

"Here? Just now? One of your neighbours might have a heart attack."

Sylvia laughed. "I hope you'll let me see it sometime," she murmured, giving Jill a quick tug on the shoulder.

When they reached home, they poured themselves a glass of wine and prepared a light supper. It was warm outside, and Sylvia set the table on the terrace behind the house. There was a delicious stillness in the air; the world seemed at rest. The conversation while they ate became increasingly tentative, increasingly intermittent. Each was lost in her own thoughts. In the approaching darkness, there was not a breath of wind, not even in the treetops. Nature was on hold: the atmosphere was one of expectation.

Sylvia felt a wonderful feeling rising within her, a feeling of wellbeing. She knew in her own mind that in Jill, she had at last found the right person, and that a great experience lay ahead of her. She edged her chair closer to Jill's, seeking her warmth and complicity. Jill sensed the rising excitement in Sylvia and felt one building in herself as well.

They remained there in the quiet of the evening, relishing the moment. When the light finally faded, Jill reached over to Sylvia's lap. Their hands closed together. Wordlessly, they rose, and after sharing a long embrace, they went indoors.

5

"Are you alright?" he asks. Jessica is standing there in the middle of the road, looking down at her bicycle. She is red-headed and skinny. John particularly notices her freckles. "You have a flat tire."

"I know," says Jessica. "I hit a hole. That one there," she says, pointing at the road behind her.

"Did you hurt yourself?" He notices the dirt on her left leg, a long scratch, a bit of blood.

"It's nothing," she says, looking down at her leg. "You are John Cowan, aren't you?" In fact, she knows perfectly well who he is. It's just that he is three years ahead of her at school. He's about to graduate. She is only fourteen. That's a big difference.

"Yes, and you are Jessica Symons. You live in the big house." Today, Jessica does not appear to him like the little girl he has occasionally noticed at school. Here, there is only her; she stands out. At school, she is one of a number of the younger girls all off by themselves, laughing and chattering.

Jessica attempts to straighten up. "Ouch!" she says. The small amount of blood on her leg has clotted and started to dry. It hurts a bit when she moves. "What's that in your box?"

she asks.

John is a bit bashful. "Specimens," he says.

"Specimens of what?"

"Insects. Butterflies. Flowers. Whatever I can find." He is afraid that she will think he's a nerd.

"Show me," she demands.

He carefully opens the little box, not wanting to lose any of its contents. She leans close, in order to see. The mass of her long red hair swings towards him and brushes against his shoulder. John feels strange, uncomfortable. "There's not much to see."

"What will you do with them now?" Jessica asks.

"At home I have several books, on plants, on insects, all that. I identify what I find and make lists."

Jessica picks up her bike. "I should go home now. Will you come with me?"

"I'm going in that direction as well. We can go together."

"Do you mind if I put my hand on your shoulder? My leg hurts a bit." Jessica doesn't wait for an answer. Her left hand reaches up to John's shoulder, and with her right hand, she grasps her bike by the handlebars.

Neither has yet called the other by name. They start back along the road. It is little more than a narrow country lane, hemmed in by hedges and fields. It is midsummer and the birds are singing.

6

John Cowan was sitting on the roof of Tessie's house in Makkovik, a small village on the Atlantic coast of central Labrador. He was in his fifties, tall and strongly built. He had a handsome, angular face and untidy brown hair that kept falling over his eyes so that he had to brush it back periodically with his hand.

It was a sunny morning at the end of August, and from his vantage point, John had a great view of the bay and of the ocean beyond. Closer at hand were the fish packing plant and the wharf where the long liners would come in to unload their catches of turbot and halibut.

John held several asphalt shingles in his left hand and, with his right, lowered a rope down to where Tessie was standing so that she could attach a pot of sticky black adhesive.

"It's really kind of you to be doing this, John. I can't thank you enough."

"A pleasure, Tessie. It's always good to see you and being up here takes me back to my construction days in Goose Bay."

When John had first came out from Scotland almost thirty years previously, he settled in Happy Valley-Goose Bay, Labrador's only large town, where he found a job doing maintenance work at the hospital. He soon started a construction business of his own and did pretty well, building small houses and eventually larger commercial buildings.

He then sold out, and tried his hand at prospecting, looking for uranium in particular. He spent summers going up rivers in his canoe with a tent, an axe, a rifle, a fishing rod, and supplies of lard, flour, tea, sugar and little else. He did this for several years and got to know a number of the rivers up the Labrador coast north of Goose Bay: Michael's River, the Kanairiktok, the Notakwanon, the Adlatok - all big rivers. It was hard work and he covered a lot of ground, but he never found minerals in sufficient concentration to justify staking a claim.

He met his wife Melba during these years. They were married in the Moravian church in Hopedale. They then moved down the coast to Makkovik, which then counted about three hundred inhabitants, and John was granted a government lease of a spot on the Big River where he proceeded to build their home.

"All finished," John shouted down to Tessie. "Hold the ladder, I'm coming down."

"What were you doing in Goose Bay?" she asked him when he reached the ground.

"I had to agree a lease with a new tenant. You remember my building near the hospital? There's already a pharmacy and a dentist's office. Now there's going to be a physiotherapist."

Tessie invited John inside to get cleaned up and have a cup of tea, and they enjoyed a bit of a chat.

"That's a good picture of you and Ernie," John said, looking at a photo on the wall. Tessie's husband had died three years previously. It had been a great loss, as they had been very close to John and his wife Melba. Ernest was a judge, and originally came from the Island, as Newfoundland was known up in Labrador. They and their two children had often come down in their motorboat to visit the Cowans at their house on the Big River.

"Do you remember the great games of bridge we used to play?" Tessie asked, sipping her tea thoughtfully.

"And those long summer nights," John added with a smile, "discussing natural justice and Ernie's court cases."

After a few minutes, John looked at his watch, said that it was time to go, and headed off down the hill towards where his boat was tied up. He had already been to the general store and the boat was loaded with three boxes of groceries, a fresh tank of propane and the mail. The tide was just right, the weather fair, and he reckoned he could be home by seven, just in time for dinner.

On his way down, he stopped by the Moravian church, a simple but handsome white building with a long history behind it. Two hundred and fifty years back, Moravian missionaries had come out from central Europe to the Labrador coast, setting up schools and providing support to the local communities. Their white wooden churches could still be seen standing in coastal villages such as Hopedale and Makkovik. Outside the church was a sign with the Moravian motto:

"In essentials, unity.
In non-essentials, liberty.
In all other things, love."

Each time he passed this way, John would reread the motto. It nicely summarised his own feelings about life.

He untied the boat, put on his life jacket, started up the engine and was on his way. The trip down the coast was one that he always enjoyed: speeding off across the water gave him an exhilarating sense of freedom and of happiness.

It was ten to seven when John arrived home. The house was located on the north side of the river, where it had narrowed to about three hundred metres. The current was very strong here, even when the tide was rising, as it was at present, and the dock was firmly attached with ropes to some birch trees on the bank of the river. Melba stood there on the dock, stretching out her arms to welcome her man, and beside her was Sheila, slim and smiling, her dark hair falling down in a braid to the middle of her back. David then came leaping down the wooden steps which led from above, and with a cheerful "Hi, Dad," picked up the heaviest box in the boat and carried it up to the house.

At the top of the steps was a short lawn and several wooden buildings. The house itself was on one floor and painted dark green. A wide porch fronted onto the river, with screening on part of it to keep out the mosquitos and black flies. The building was set on a number of wooden supports, spruce logs sunk into the soil below.

The gap between the house and the ground was filled by a neat white lattice. A set of stairs led up to the porch and two fishing rods lay in racks to one side. John followed the others into the house. There was a delicious smell of softwood smoke in the air, and supper was soon on the table.

John considered himself to be very fortunate. He loved his wife and he loved his children. His life was in equilibrium, each part fitting neatly into the next. Only occasionally did his thoughts wander back to his early days in Scotland.

7

Duncan collapsed into an armchair in his mother's living room and looked around. The room seemed dreary to him: all those objects from the past, all that mauve and brown.

He could hear his mother moving about upstairs. Rather than calling up to her, he decided to wait below, in silence. She would be coming down soon enough.

He rose and looked at himself in a mirror. Thinning red hair. "I'm going bald," he thought. A pale, slightly flabby face. Circles under his eyes. Too much of a beer belly.

He was tired, not so much from physical exertion as from ennui. His life was dull and repetitive, without any sharp edges. Boring days at the bank, days that never seemed to come to an end, were followed by long solitary evenings at home and sleepless nights. Everything was touched by a common greyness.

The door swung open, and his mother appeared. "Duncan!" she exclaimed. "I didn't hear you arrive." She came up to him to give him a kiss, and he returned her kiss gallantly enough. They then both sat down.

"Tell me about yourself," Mary said. "Are you getting enough to eat? You look to me as if you have lost a bit of weight."

The image she had of Duncan ran back twenty-five years or more, when he was fresh out of the army, handsome and fit, and still unmarried. The reality today was less prepossessing

"Oh, don't worry about me, Mum. I'm getting by."

"Poor darling," she continued. "What do you do for dinner? Perhaps you should come here and I could make something up for the two of us."

"I have things brought to me at home," Duncan said quickly. "Pizzas, Chinese, curry, that sort of thing. It doesn't work out all that badly."

Mary was far from convinced, but let the matter drop. "Any news of the children?" she asked. Duncan's wife Ruth had left him some months ago with their three children. She was now living in Glasgow, with another man it seemed, and Duncan only rarely received news from her.

"No," was his short answer. He sometimes wondered what, if anything, he could do about it. Ruth would bring the children up her own way, and all in all she was a good mother. Probably, the children didn't even miss their father. Later on in life, as they became independent, he would have to establish new relationships with each of them. He was occasionally tormented by the thought that perhaps he had never been a particularly good father to his children. Was that possible? Was he really that cold, that heartless? Or had it only been due to his deteriorating relationship with Ruth?

"Let's hope that they're alright," said his mother. "Perhaps you should go down to Glasgow to visit them." She thought that now would be the time to bring up the question that was really on her mind. "Sylvia came to see me yesterday," she said.

"She's well, I hope."

"Very well, it seems. Just now she has a friend visiting from Glasgow. Her name is Jill. I haven't met her, but she sounds very nice."

"Does Sylvia still have that job with the fish wholesaler in

Aberdeen?"

"Yes. She works mostly from home."

Duncan stared out the window.

"Syl and I discussed John," Mary continued, "and how wonderful it would be for all of us if we could convince him to come back for a visit."

Duncan had long ago written his brother off, so that when his mother brought the subject up, as she frequently did, he tended to listen in silence.

"I know that we have asked John to come on many occasions," Mary added. "Soon, however, it will be too late. I'm not immortal."

Duncan looked at his mother. The poor dear, she really was showing her age: those wrinkles at the neck, the difficulties rising from her chair, the increasing shortness of breath. A touch of sadness came over him, a feeling of regret. "So, you plan to write him again? Would you like each of us to add a little note?"

"No," she said energetically. "I have a much better idea." She paused. "I think that you yourself should go out to Canada to convince John."

Duncan started up. "Mother, you can't be serious!"

"I am," she said. "In fact, I am asking you to do so, on my behalf." She corrected herself. "On all of our behalves."

Duncan rubbed his chin with his hand. "Was this Sylvia's doing?" he wondered. "I can't go off to Canada, Mum," he said. "I have to work."

"I'm sure you could sort something out with the bank. In any event, haven't you some vacation days coming to you?"

"Well yes, but..."

"It could make for a very interesting trip. Remember how much you enjoyed your stay in Brazil. Labrador must be just as interesting as Brazil, if not even more so."

Duncan managed a weak smile. "I think that the beaches would be different. Also, the girls..."

"Wouldn't you like to see your brother again and meet your nephew and your niece?"

Duncan shrugged. "I suppose."

Mary became impatient. "Come on, Duncan. Buck up! Smile a bit. What's wrong with you?"

Duncan remained silent for a while. How could he smile when he was feeling so rotten? "What makes you think that John would agree?" he finally asked.

Mary replied vigorously. "I'm sure of it."

"But Mum, he's been refusing to come for over thirty years. What would make him come now?" Duncan was not at all happy with this idea of his mother's. He had any number of reasons to find it inconvenient. He was seriously considering quitting his job at the bank and would have to start right away looking for something else to replace it. He needed to sort out his marriage with Ruth. Above all, at the present time, he felt emotionally and physically exhausted.

"Darling," his mother replied, "it would be such a dramatic event, your showing up like that in Labrador. John would have to take the matter very seriously and you would have a special card to play: you could tell him that I was yearning to see him and that I was not eternal."

The thought brought sudden tears to Mary's eyes. Duncan softened. He always gave way to a woman's tears. Why was that? Was it because he couldn't bear to hurt a woman, or on the contrary, because he felt confirmed in a feeling of masculine strength and superiority? Was it simply because he was weak? He just didn't know.

Duncan paused. He couldn't think of a good reason to refuse his mother. "All right, Mum. I'll go," he said reluctantly. "I wouldn't do it for any other person, but for you, I'll do it."

8

Sylvia wanted her mother and Jill to meet, so early the next week she and Jill set off for the city in Sylvia's grey Prius. They were both a bit tired, but otherwise very upbeat.

When they reached Mary's house in Old Aberdeen, they found her sitting in her usual armchair, looking out the window. The top of one of the massive towers of Saint Machar's kirk loomed above the houses across the way. Mary loved that church, it seemed so emblematic of Scotland itself: strong, austere, ancient.

"Hello, Mum," Sylvia said cheerily. "How are you doing? I've brought a special visitor for you." With that, she introduced Jill, and the two pulled up chairs for a chat.

"It's very good to meet you, Jill," said Mary. "Sylvia has been telling me a lot about you."

Jill smiled. "I hope she left out all my bad habits."

Mary laughed. "She never even tells me about her own. How do you find living out at Ardeath? I gather you were previously a city girl."

"I love it up here. Living with Syl is a new experience. The countryside is lovely. I'm getting far more exercise than I used to. Syl's cottage is totally charming. Mary - I hope I may call

37

you Mary - I think I'm very lucky, and I don't miss Glasgow a single bit."

"I'm delighted to hear that, and yes, please do call me Mary. Have you found yourself a job? Syl told me you had something in mind."

"Yes, and I start next Monday. It's only part time for now, at the Post Office in Ellon."

Mary was instantly drawn to Jill. "Good for Syl," she said to herself. "I think the two are very well suited."

Sylvia now returned from the kitchen where she had been making them a pot of tea. "Have you had any news from Duncan?" she asked her mother.

"Not really. I think he's in Saint John's right now, but he should be up in Labrador in a day or so." Mary's face took on a far-away look. "Oh, won't it be wonderful to see John again!"

Sylvia looked up at her. "Hang on, Mum. Just because Duncan's on his way doesn't mean that John will agree to come back."

"Of course, he will," was the confident reply. How could he refuse his own mother? After all those years? In spite of everything. A silence came over the three of them.

"What's new out at Ardeath?" Mary finally asked.

"Nothing much. The barley is pretty much all in. They're still making a bit of silage on some of the farms. Keith is making a few repairs on the estate, here and there."

"How do you think Keith makes both ends meet out there in the big house?" Mary asked. "He doesn't farm himself and the rents from the estate can't add up to all that much. That house of his must cost a fortune to heat."

"He has been selling off bits of land down by the village," said Sylvia. "Then he puts down two thousand pheasants each year and lets a few days' shooting to a syndicate of oilmen from Aberdeen. Also, I understand that Georgie has a bit of money of her own." Georgie was how everyone referred to Keith's Dutch wife, Georgina.

Sylvia didn't really approve of let shooting, because it entailed rearing hundreds of birds like so many chickens, releasing them into nature when they were not fully grown, and hiring a number of beaters to drive them over a line of men holding expensive guns.

Mary thought the same way. "Those let days of shooting are a nightmare," she said. "People getting hit by spent pellets and shooting at birds that are so close they blow them to bits."

She turned to Jill. "I used to like rough shooting most; my husband was an excellent shot and used to go out on a Saturday with his friends. I often went along with them to pick up, particularly when I had Jess, who was the best dog in the business. Has Sylvia taken you out to see the mosses above the village?"

"No. Not yet."

"In any event, that's where we used to go: on the mosses. There might be ten or fifteen men carrying guns, and others of us with dogs, and we would walk abreast for hours on end. You never knew what the next shot might be: rabbit, snipe, woodcock, hare, pheasant, pigeon, duck. Even grouse. We walked all day, sun or rain, until our legs just about collapsed, because it was rough walking on those soft, spongy mosses. There was a pond towards the middle of the moss where we used to stop for lunch. It had a single exhausted-looking willow at one end, and we all used to sit under it eating our sandwiches surrounded by smelly wet dogs."

"More reminiscences," thought Sylvia. "Oh well. Jill seems interested."

Mary spoke once more to Jill. "This isn't my country, Jill. My family was a fishing family. I was born in Inverallochy, some fifty miles up the coast. My father's name was Christie. At home we spoke Doric, and the men made their living fishing for cod and plaice out there on the North Sea, which my grandfather used to call the German Ocean. And now, here's my son John, emigrated to Canada. What a change!"

Sylvia and Jill eventually took their leave and headed back to Ardeath. They came to the village, which consisted of a number of little stone houses, all very neat and tidy, gathered around a square. To one side was a triangular pond, fed by a small stream that came down from the mosses and in turn ran out of the village to join up with a small northern tributary of the Ythan river. By the pond was the village pub, and they went in for a glass of lager.

Sylvia recognised a few faces and introduced Jill to one or two local celebrities, including Jock, the retired water bailiff, and Sandy Mitchell, gamekeeper on the Ardeath estate. Jock was a tall, distinguished looking man with silver hair and a tweed cap, which he kept on all the time. Sandy was stocky, his bulk emphasised by the fact that he wore baggy tweed breeches, a flannel shirt, and a woolen tie. Sandy joined them at their table, and Sylvia told Jill and Sandy how she and Duncan had once gone fishing with Jock on the Ythan.

"Once, many years ago," she said, "when we were living at Bonnycastle, Jock came over to the house and gave Mum a big sea trout. Duncan and I were there, and Jock asked us if we would like to go fishing that evening. It was the thirty-first day of October, the last day of the season."

"After supper, Duncan borrowed Mum's car, and we took two rods and went down to meet Jock on a stretch of the river. I was in exams, I think. In any event, I was really tired. Jock put two flies on our lines. 'Two killers,' he said. He set us up on two different spots of the riverbank. We started fishing, and it got darker and darker. At the end, you could only guess where the river was. But Jock was determined that we should catch something, if necessary remaining there right up to the end of the season, the stroke of midnight. He didn't fish himself; he just ran back and forth between us, saying 'put your fly here, put it there' and so forth. At about nine-thirty, I caught a branch behind me. I was just too tired to go back into the bushes to sort things out, so I let out a bit of line and each time

Jock came by, I would go swish-swish with my rod, as though I was casting. I reckoned that if I couldn't see what was going on, Jock wouldn't be able to either."

"What happened at midnight?" Jill asked.

"I don't know. I was sound asleep!" The three laughed. Sylvia and Jill emptied their glasses, said goodbye to Sandy and returned to the car.

"I liked Sandy," Jill said. "So, he works at Ardeath?"

"Yes, he has been gamekeeper there for I don't know how many years. I sometimes wonder how he gets on with Keith Symons, who is hardly the most charming man you will ever meet. It's just a job, I suppose."

"How old do you think Sandy is?"

"He must be in his sixties. I seem to remember that he even worked at Ardeath for Keith's father."

"The man who died in the shooting accident?"

"Yes. Gerald Symons."

"If it was an accident," Jill said thoughtfully. "Tell me, Syl," she said. "Would it bother you if I made a little investigation into the circumstances surrounding Gerald Symons' death?"

"Why not? That way, you could even make it clear that John wasn't involved."

"Yes I could. There's something there that makes me wonder, something that might be different from what everyone has thought until now. It might even be material for a new article."

Sylvia thought for a moment. "An article about Gerald's death? I don't know," she said. "That could be tricky. It would depend on what you found out, I suppose."

"I would certainly keep you informed, and if, for whatever reason, you became uneasy with what emerged, I would stop right there."

Sylvia smiled. "All right, Jill. Go ahead. Just as long as it doesn't become too sensitive for us all, for whatever reason."

"Of course. Thanks for your confidence in me, and I

promise that I'll keep you fully informed."

The sky had become a dull grey and the wind was picking up. Rain was on its way. The weather in this part of Scotland, in Buchan as it was known, was always like this. It was constantly changing and could catch you by surprise. They reached the cottage just before the rain started.

9

Jessica looked around her little shop at the top of Union Street. It was depressing. The flower business was tough at this time because of the pandemic. There were no receptions, no marriages or funerals, not even any church services. So, she operated with a reduced inventory and the shop shelves were half empty. She met few clients in the flesh but did most of her business by phone or through the internet.

She often found herself delivering flowers herself and blessed the day she had replaced her car by a Volkswagen van, which was much sturdier. She had bought it second-hand, and it had been repainted with her logo on the two sides. It looked very smart.

Jessica had just turned fifty, was single, and singularly beautiful. If she had things on her mind, it certainly didn't show. She wore her auburn hair shoulder length; it had gentle curls and was swept back above a high forehead. Her eyebrows arched above slate grey eyes. They were only sometimes grey, as they tended to pick up those shades of green or blue that happened to be at hand. Her nose was straight and led down to a mouth that was full, but not very wide, so that at times, when the lips were closed, they seemed to form an oval.

Just then, the phone rang. "Good afternoon," she answered. "Jessica's Flowers. Can I help you?"

There was a pause, then a woman's voice asked if she could purchase some flowers and have them delivered to an address in Old Aberdeen.

"With pleasure. We have some very nice roses, also chrysanthemums and delphinium. I recommend the roses. We have white and pink, and mixed together they look super."

"That sounds fine," said the caller. "I'll take a dozen please. They're for a lady who lives in Old Aberdeen and is not in the best of health."

"That's nice of you! Could I please have her name, telephone number and address."

"Yes, certainly. They're for a Mrs Mary Cowan. Her address is 41b Don Street and her telephone number is 462 844."

Jessica paused for a moment. The name Mary Cowan seemed very familiar. There had been a Mary Cowan living on Ardeath when Jessica was a child. She wondered if there might be a connection. "I'll deliver them tomorrow," she said. "Is that alright?"

"That would be perfect."

"Would you like me to attach a card?"

"Yes, for sure. Just say with love from Syl and Jill."

"Syl spelled s - y - l?"

"Yes, as in Sylvia."

Jessica stopped writing. Old associations started to race through her head. Mary Cowan - wasn't Mary the name of John's mother? And Sylvia - that surely was the name of his sister. Her heart pounded as memories of John came flooding back. She asked for the caller's credit card details, and the caller gave an address in Glasgow. "Are you calling from Glasgow?" she asked.

"No. I've just moved up here," was the reply. "I live outside Ellon."

Jessica couldn't contain her curiosity. "Do you mind if I ask you something?" She flicked a curl off her forehead. "Is Sylvia's last name Cowan? I used to know a family named Cowan very well. There was Sylvia, and Duncan, and…"

"Yes, my friend is Sylvia Cowan, and her mother's name is Mary. She has two brothers, John and Duncan. They must be the same persons."

Jessica felt the excitement rising within her. John! She couldn't believe her ears. "My name's Jessica. Jessica Symons. We all lived together out at Ardeath, long ago. I lived in the big house," she said almost apologetically, "and the Cowans were at one of the farms, Bonnycastle. I'd love to see them again." She didn't want the conversation to end but didn't know what more to say.

"I'm Jill. Jill Brown. I'll tell Sylvia that I spoke to you."

"Please, though, before you hang up. Tell me about them. What is their news? I would so much like to know."

"Well, Mary is getting on in age, as I think I said before. Sylvia is very well; I have just started to live with her in her cottage at Ardeath, more or less next to Bonnycastle. Duncan and John, I have not met. Duncan lives here in Aberdeen, and John lives in Canada, where he emigrated a long time ago. He has never been back, but Duncan has just gone out there to convince him to return for a visit."

Jessica twisted a length of hair around her finger. "That would be marvellous! I mean, if John comes back for a visit. Where will he stay?"

"We don't actually know yet whether he will agree to come. But my understanding is that if he does come, he will stay with his mother, with Mary."

"For how long?"

"Probably three weeks. That's the plan in any case."

"Please tell Sylvia we spoke. Perhaps we could get together some time. I'm so happy you called, Jill. I'll be around at Mary's tomorrow with the roses."

"That's just fine, Jessica. What a coincidence! Mary will be happy to see you, I'm sure."

"Goodbye, Jill."

"Goodbye, Jessica."

After the call, Jessica remained seated, lost in her thoughts, her memories.

10

She is waiting for him beside the old, abandoned cottage where they sometimes meet. It's their secret place. From there they can walk out across the fields all by themselves, unobserved. "Hi, Jess," comes a low voice from nearby. It's John! Her heart skips a beat and off they go.

They are both warmly dressed as the year is coming to a close. They cross a small field, jump a barbed-wire fence, and now can talk normally without fear of being heard.

"Sorry I'm a bit late. I was feeding the cattle."

"That's OK. I hadn't been there for long."

"Is school going well?" John asks.

Jessica makes a face. "One more year to go; after this one, I mean. I can't wait."

"Stick at it," John says. "It's important. Have you thought of what you want to do afterwards?" he asks.

"Travel," is the answer. "I'd like to travel, to take a long trip somewhere." A rabbit suddenly appears out of a tuft of grass at their feet and disappears across the field like quicksilver. "Like that rabbit," she laughs.

John smiles at the analogy. "In any event, I have decided that I don't want to be a farmer all my life." At the present time, he is working on the farm helping his father.

"Do you still intend to go to university?" Jessica asks. She feels threatened by the thought of his doing so. Even if she knows that it would suit him.

"Possibly. I'm trying to save up a bit. Look at those lapwings," he says, pointing at a small flock of birds wheeling in the air above a nearby bit of wet ground. "Let's go over there to see what they are finding so interesting." They go through a gate into the next field.

The lapwings disappear before they reach the spot, giving their characteristic cry. John and Jessica are now walking in barley stubble and their boots make a curious popping noise as they go along. Jessica loves that noise. "I would be happy walking in the barley stubble with John for the rest of my life," she thinks to herself.

John picks up a head of barley that the combine missed. "Golden Promise," he explains. "One of the best strains. Good quality and a fairly heavy crop."

They come to a long row of bales of golden straw that the farmer has neatly put along the edge of the field. John leans on a bale and removes a boot to shake something out that is annoying him. Jessica looks at him; he is tall and gangly. Slightly awkward. However, in her eyes, he is everything. Her eyes go slightly misty; she can't hold back. She jumps at him, wraps her arms around his unsuspecting body, and kisses him.

At first, he is startled, but then he holds her close and kisses her back, first on her lips, then the tip of the nose, then the forehead, on each cheek, on the lips again. They are both laughing, and they kiss each other again, again and again. They are drowning in the intoxication of first love.

11

Duncan stood on the deck of the *Kamutik* and looked back at Otter Creek and Goose Bay as they receded into the distance. The ship was vibrating with a deep hum from the engine room and started to heave as they reached deeper water. "This trip is turning out to be quite interesting," he thought. "Much more so than I had expected."

It wasn't sea as Duncan knew it, not like the North Sea lying off the coast of Aberdeenshire. In fact, Goose Bay lay well in from the Atlantic, at the westernmost extremity of a very deep inlet from the open sea. As the *Kamutik* made its way east and north towards its first stop, Rigolet, it passed along a shoreline of wooded mountains and sandy beaches. Rafts of black duck rose from the water ahead of the ship, disappearing behind rocky islets and reappearing again high in the sky, headed for who knew where. Minke whales could be seen occasionally, porpoising happily nearby the vessel.

It became cold outside and Duncan sought comfort in the lounge of the *Kamutik*, purchasing a rather unappetising sandwich and rolling himself up in his coat for a night's sleep. There weren't that many other passengers; they were mostly native, both Inuit and Innu.

Shortly before midnight, they made a brief stop at Rigolet, a town of about three hundred inhabitants. There was a floodlit wharf, a few twinkling lights beyond and then nothing, a black void, the endless Labrador wilderness.

The sun was beginning to rise when Duncan awoke. The *Kamutik* was making heavy going. They were now out into the Atlantic, and the swell had become insistent, compelling, even menacing. Elsewhere in the lounge, the other passengers were clustered in groups around their bags and boxes and were beginning to stir. Duncan himself had only a medium-sized packsack. He was travelling light but was beginning to realise that he would need more to stay warm, perhaps a rain jacket and even some boots. Hopefully, he would find them in Makkovik.

On deck there was a fierce wind out of the northwest. Leaning on the port rail was a short man in rain gear from head to foot. Donald approached him, attaching himself to the rail some five feet away, and gave him a good morning.

"And good morning to you," said the man. "Where are you headed?"

"Makkovik. What a cold wind! Is it always like this? My name's Duncan," he said. "Duncan Cowan."

"Obliged. Bill Kane. I'm also going to Makkovik. What takes you there?"

"My brother lives there, at least near there at a place called the Big River."

Bill's eyes lit up. "I know the Big River. It's a beauty. There are a lot of good char brooks along that bit of coast."

"Arctic char? I have eaten char in the restaurant, but I must say I don't know much about them. I don't even know what a char looks like."

"Like a salmon, but more colour. Char spawn and overwinter in the ponds inland, and come down to salt water in the spring and through the summer, when you can fish for them off the rocks and along the beach. They can get pretty big, as big as a salmon, and they jump a lot when you hook 'em, but they have less staying power than the salmon."

Duncan was no angler and thought that he would change the subject. "Do you live in Makkovik?"

"Yes, I'm a teacher there. But I'm originally from the Island, from Newfoundland."

Just then, there was a commotion on the other side of the *Kamutik*, and they both looked across to see what it might be. A few other passengers were on deck, pointing excitedly to an iceberg about a quarter of a mile from the ship, and close to one third its size. It was the first iceberg that Duncan had ever seen. In fact, it was one of the most beautiful sights that he had ever seen. It floated above the dark ocean, the palest of turquoise in the morning sun, with a seam of deep blue running through it from one end to the other. Its surface had been smoothed by waves and rain, giving it the look of a cabochon gemstone. It regularly heaved up in the waves, water pouring off its flanks; it would then sink slowly back down into the sea again, in a constant cycle as if it was a living organism.

Duncan stood there looking at the iceberg. He was fascinated. Where did it come from? Where was it going? How long would it last before it melted? It made him think about himself. Who was he? Where was he going? Was his marriage finished? What was his future?

Just before leaving, he had given notice to leave his job at the bank. Eight years working in Compliance were more than enough. What should he do now? That was the question.

There was one possibility, and the more he thought about it, the more it appealed to him. His mother's brother, Gordon Christie, had been a fisherman all his life. Although his uncle came from Inverallochy, at a young age, he had moved into nearby Fraserburgh at the tip of the knuckle of Buchan. The Broch, as Fraserburgh was called locally, was an important fishing port, one of the most important in the whole of Europe.

Gordon Christie had acquired a trawler called the *Sunset Sea* and operated it in partnership with his two sons for many prosperous years. Now that he was getting on in years, he had let it be known to his sister Mary that if ever Duncan wished to buy his share in the vessel, he and his two sons would be in favour of the transaction.

"Yes," he said to himself as the *Kamutik* gradually made its way up the coast towards Makkovik. "When I return to Aberdeenshire, I'll speak to my uncle Gordon."

Duncan suddenly realised that for whatever reason, he was once more feeling like a human being.

12

Duncan shouldered his packsack and set out for a stroll around Makkovik. It was about the same size as Rigolet, prosperous enough and very well kept up. He passed the fish-packing plant and turning along the shore came to an area known as Little Hebron where in the late 1950s, the government had resettled a number of families living hundreds of miles up the coast in a place called Hebron. Strewn about in friendly disorder were stacks of firewood, modern aluminum boats and old wooden dinghies, ski-doos in various states of repair, wooden sleds, and a variety of houses, some of recent and some of not-so-recent construction. There were pickup trucks and the odd car, and any number of quad bikes, but what really struck him was the number of ski-doos. Clearly, they were the only means of travel once the snow came.

Duncan had soon seen all that there was to see. However, he realised that as he walked along the edge of the bay he had been treated to a constant serenade of dogs barking and howling. There they were now in front of him, next to a small creek as it fed into the salt water, seven or eight in number, each attached by a very stout chain to eye bolts fixed in the bare rocks. With them was a slight, round-faced man with jet-black hair and a large moustache. He gave a bright smile and had wonderfully white teeth. On the streets of Aberdeen, he would have been mistaken as being Japanese.

"Hello Skipper! What do you think of 'em? Have you ever seen better huskies?"

"I don't know much about huskies," Duncan replied. He noticed that even though the man had ventured close to his dogs as he talked to them, he made a point of remaining very calm, very careful. Duncan came up to where he was standing in order to get a better view.

"This one here with the white fur, it has mostly Siberian blood. These ones here, with the big heads and broad, black foreheads, they are Labradorian."

The Labradorians looked particularly sinister to Duncan, like so many wolves. "Do they have any wolf in them?" he asked.

"Yes, a bit," said his new companion. "Wolf blood in a dog can give it greater speed and stamina, but the shoulder bones on a wolf are separated, and can be injured by the harness. Also, wolves are wilder. So, if you breed wolf into your huskies, it's better to wait three generations before using the puppies to pull a sled."

"And do you use them to pull a sled?" asked Duncan, feeling a bit stupid, but he didn't quite know what else to say.

"For sure!" exclaimed the man, straightening up. "There's a big gathering here on the Labrador coast every March. We race our dogs against each other and sometimes even against foreign teams. With one team, I placed third overall last year."

Duncan noticed that his new friend had referred to "one team". "Did you race a second team as well?" he asked.

The man grinned, his white teeth gleaming like snow. "Yes, I did, but we got into a fight with another team," he said, "and it was a hell of a job to separate them."

Duncan laughed. "That must have been quite something!"

"It's too bad though," said the man, the regret showing on

his face. "There aren't so many teams today as there used to be. Those days are going fast."

As it was time to think about the reason he was here in Makkovik, Duncan took the plunge. "Do you mind if I ask you something?"

"Not at all," said the man. "How can I help you? My name's Charlie, Charlie Webb."

"My name's Duncan Cowan. I come from Scotland and I'm here to look for my brother John. He is in his mid-fifties, and the only thing I know about his whereabouts is that he lives on the Big River."

Charlie thought for a while. "I would be happy to help you, but I've never heard tell of your brother. However, that's no problem. We can go down to see Uncle Joe - everyone calls him that, he's not my uncle at all - he used to be a trapper and knows every bit of the coast near here. If your brother lives down by the Big River, Uncle Joe will know about him."

Charlie gave a last look at his huskies, and then the two of them set off back towards the centre of the village, soon finding themselves in front of a neat white house with a low picket fence between it and the roadside. Beside it was a shed with its door open, and inside it Duncan could see two big ski-doos, a small red canoe and assorted gear. A big man with dirty overalls was moving about. He had tousled grey hair with a little black tuque perched on top, and a full red beard. He seemed a happy man, as he was singing a little song to himself.

"Old Mister Milligan down by the Billigan stream.
He peed for an hour and a quarter,
And you couldn't see his belly for the steam."

"Hello, Uncle Joe," shouted Charlie, "and how's the missus?"

"Hello there, Charlie. Why, she's just fine thanks, and

how's yourself?" Uncle Joe wiped his hands on some paper towel.

"Not bad. This man here's got a question for you."

Uncle Joe straightened up with a smile and looked at Duncan. "And what might that be, my son?"

Duncan looked at Uncle Joe. "Have you ever come across a man called John Cowan, about fifty-five years old. He's my brother and I want to catch up with him."

Uncle Joe didn't hesitate for a moment. "Sure, if he's the man I'm thinking of. Lives down the coast a bit, on the Big River." He turned to Charlie. "He's married to Melba, Johnnie's daughter."

"Johnnie Smail?"

"That's the one."

Charlie turned to Duncan. "Well, that was easy. We've found your brother, alright."

"He has a green house with a big deck, on the north shore of the river, just above salt water," added Uncle Joe.

"Does he have an accent?" Duncan asked Uncle Joe, wishing to make sure they were talking about the same person. "A Scottish accent, like mine?"

"Sort of, I guess, but he's now learned to talk properly." Duncan let that one pass.

"And now what?" asked Charlie, turning to Duncan. "Do you want to go down the coast to the Big River to look for him?"

"I would love to, but how can I do so?"

"I can take you, as long as the sea is quiet. It's the wind these days. The sea can get pretty rough."

"I can pay you," Duncan offered. He feared Charlie might be offended, but it didn't seem to be a problem. "You just let me know. I don't know how these things work around here."

Charlie was already thinking about the trip. "The tide will be right tomorrow morning at four o'clock. The wind is supposed to drop. Do you have the right clothes?" he asked, looking doubtfully at Duncan. "It can get very cold out there on the water."

"Have you boots?" Uncle Joe asked in turn, looking hard at Duncan's shoes. He disappeared into the back of the shed and reappeared with an old pair of grey thigh-waders, the kind commercial fishermen wear. "These should fit."

"I have an extra set of heavy rain gear," Charlie said.

"And I have a woolen tuque and some mitts," Duncan added.

"Then you're all set," said Uncle Joe, eying Duncan, "and when you get back from the Big River, bring along a bottle of screech and we'll split the difference." Duncan thought he understood, and nodded cheerfully. After all, he was on his way to the Big River and to finding his brother John.

13

They were already at Charlie's boat at three-thirty the next morning. Duncan had slept on Charlie's living room couch, surrounded by old photographs, ribbons won in sled races, an outdated TV and a lot of mugs and china cups hung in rows. Apparently, there was a Mrs Charlie, but she was up the coast visiting her sister.

Just how Charlie could see anything in the dark outside was a complete mystery, but by ten to four, they were pulling out of the bay and heading east. The boat was an open boat, built of aluminum and about eighteen feet long. Charlie stood in the stern, one hand on the handle of a thirty-five horsepower outboard engine, and the other holding a short rope that was attached to the seat in front of him and which steadied his balance. In the bottom of the boat were three extra reservoirs of fuel, two anchors, ropes, tarps, oars, a rifle wrapped in some tarp, an axe, and Duncan's bag.

As they bored on through the night, heading north and east on quiet water at close to full throttle, with a clear September sky full of stars overhead, Duncan was overwhelmed by a sense of solitude, of space, of freedom, such as he had never experienced before. It gave rise to a feeling within him which he found difficult to explain and over which he had no control. It made him intensely happy, even elated. He had not felt this way for a very, very long time, if ever.

Rosy-fingered dawn was soon upon them, and they rounded a barren rocky headland and turned to the south. After a while, Charlie throttled back and made a sign for Duncan to come to the back of the boat and take over from him. He was stiff and wanted to stretch. He showed Duncan how to handle the outboard and waved his hand vaguely off to the south, saying, "Down there's Kikkertavak island. We want to get there eventually, but we don't want to leave the shore too far on our right, so hold Kikkertavak at about eleven o'clock and take it easy, 'cause the swell picks up a bit from here on."

The swell had picked up more than a bit, but Duncan had some experience with small boats from his army days and was happy to take his turn. Charlie became talkative and pointed out various landmarks along the way.

"That's Dog Island over there," he shouted over the noise of the engine. "The little one with all the rocks. One of the boys from Makkovik used to keep his huskies there over the summer. He'd go there once or twice a week and throw some food ashore for them to eat. A lot of the boys used to do the same thing with their dogs up and down the coast. That's why there are so many Dog Islands."

"I can't see any dogs there now," Duncan shouted back, looking briefly at the island in question and shading his eyes from the morning sun.

"No. Not nowadays. There was an accident down the coast with a young girl picking berries with her family. The dogs killed her. The government then passed a law forbidding us to leave our dogs like that." Charlie fiddled with a bit of rope in the bow of the boat. "I never left my dogs loose like that. I prefer to keep them tied up. They don't get so wild, and when you want to make them work, they're so happy to be freed and put into harness that they work better.”

Duncan was fascinated. He would never have thought that in the twenty-first century, the relationship between man and dog could still be so basic, so elementary. “Tell me about Uncle Joe,” he said. “He seems quite a character.”

“Uncle Joe!” Charlie laughed. “He traps and hunts all along this coast. Trapping for beaver, marten, maybe mink. Once, he was out in the country for three or four days, and when he got back to Makkovik, he told his wife he was pretty hungry, and could do with a bowl of soup. Mrs Joe took one look at him and said ‘My God, man, you look thin! Did a bear get your grub?’. ‘No,’ he said, ‘I forgot my choppers!’”

“Meaning his axe?”

“No,” Charlie laughed. “His teeth.”

Duncan was concentrating on the sea around them, trying to hold a steady course in spite of the waves. His eyes roamed over the horizon, and he saw what looked like a fishing boat some two or three miles to their seaward side. Charlie noticed.

“That boat out there is a long-liner and is probably fishing for turbot. The turbot they catch around here are pretty small. The halibut can come a lot bigger. The catch goes back to the fish packing plant in Makkovik. That one’s a good boat. She can put out stabilisers when the sea gets rough.”

“Are all the people up here Inuit?” Duncan asked, again shouting above the noise of the engine.

“Makkovik’s an Inuit town. I’d say most of us are Inuit or mixed blood, but there are some whites as well. One family’s got Norwegian blood. Up the coast, Postville and Hopedale are also Inuit, but farther north there’s Natuashish; it’s Innu. We don’t always get along well with the Innu; they’re Naskaupi indians, a bit like the Montagnais in Quebec.”

Charlie was a veritable mine of information. Duncan asked him which town he came from.

“My family was from Hebron originally, way up in the Torngats. We moved to Makkovik in the late fifties. We were more or less forced to by the government. I think it was a good idea; life is easier down here."

"And what about Uncle Joe?" Duncan asked. "Is he Inuit?"

"Inuit, but with mixed blood. We kid him about the size of his nose. In fact, it's normal, but we kid him all the same. Once, one of the lads asked him how to get to a particular trail. It was winter, and everything was frozen. 'It's easy, my son,' said Uncle Joe. 'You go to the big pond, cross right over, and then just follow your nose.' 'That's fine Uncle Joe,' said the lad, 'but what if I turns me head?'" Charlie had a good laugh. He loved telling that one.

With stories like this, shouted over the noise of the engine, they made good time, and eventually Charlie indicated that he wished again to take control. They exchanged positions, and Charlie switched the fuel line to a new tank of gas. Duncan adjusted his life jacket, happy to be wearing it as an extra layer to protect him from the cold. Charlie brought their boat parallel to the shoreline, opened the throttle and away they went once more.

After about an hour, Charlie slowed her down a bit and seemed to be staring at a point along the shoreline. "Seal," he said. He turned the boat and they headed directly towards the shore.

Duncan looked ahead as they approached the seal. They came to about twenty metres away and he could see its round head bobbing in the waves. Suddenly, a rifle shot exploded just next to his ear: *Craaak!* He almost fell off his seat. His right ear was singing. It took him a moment before he realised what had happened.

The big seal started to sink slowly out of sight under the waves. Charlie quickly wrapped his rifle in its bit of tarp and laid it back on the floor of the boat. He then scrambled forward to give Duncan a cod-jigging line with its heavy treble hook. "See if you can snag it," he said urgently. "On the right side of the boat."

Charlie returned to the stern and brought the boat over to where the seal had disappeared. Duncan obediently threw the cod line overboard, fished about a bit and finally felt a tug. They carefully approached the shore. Twice Duncan lost the seal, and twice he snagged it again.

They reached the shore, a long strand of yellow sand. Charlie leaped into the shallows and threw the anchor into a tangle of stones and driftwood. "Hold the seal," he said. "So it doesn't float away."

Duncan held the inert seal as best he could while Charlie quickly made a ramp from the beach to the gunwales of the boat with three oars and some driftwood. "Let's go," he said. They strenuously rolled the dead seal up the ramp and over into the bow of the boat.

It had all happened very quickly, without much explanation. Charlie had taken complete control, and Duncan had followed his instructions without question. "What's the seal for?" he finally asked, somewhat lamely.

"To feed my dogs," was the answer.

Duncan felt a bit ashamed. "I should have thought of that," he said to himself.

He could hardly believe it. Here he was on this little boat somewhere out in the North Atlantic looking for a brother he hadn't seen for thirty years! "And suddenly, we shoot a seal!" he thought. "A seal!"

As Charlie took them out again along the coast, Duncan's mind turned to his brother. Wouldn't John be astonished when Duncan suddenly appeared out of nowhere! What would John be like? Would he be like the John of old, quiet, slightly intellectual, bookish even? Or would he be like Charlie, a man of action, a hunter, a child of nature? Would he welcome Duncan, or would he send him packing?

Charlie must have guessed his thoughts. "So, you're looking for your brother," he shouted. "When did you last see him?"

"Almost thirty years ago, when he first came to live here. We were brought up on a farm together. He's a couple of years older than me." Duncan was beginning to feel excited at the prospect of seeing John again.

Had they got along all that well together in their younger years? He had to admit not. John had had his own life, his own friends. And John had been to university, not so Duncan. That made a big difference. On reflection, Duncan realised that he had always been a bit envious of John, their mother's favourite, the one who took charge of family matters when their father started having his problems, the one who was closest to Sylvia even if she was nearer to Duncan in age.

Now, however, there was the possibility of starting over. Their difference in age no longer counted. It was here in Labrador that Duncan could attempt to establish a new relationship with John.

Charlie was running the boat at full throttle along the coast, his eyes searching ahead for their destination. Duncan found it a bit chummy, sitting up at the bow next to a dead seal, but by now, he was not to be surprised by anything. The seal seemed to be staring up at him, and he wondered if he should reach down and close its eyes, as they did for dead humans in the movies.

"There's not much flesh or bone on a seal," observed Charlie. "Mostly fat, but the dogs like it. Sometimes we eat the liver, if it's a young seal."

After another half hour, they seemed to be entering a broad estuary. "This is it," said Charlie, "the Big River." He stared ahead, slowing the boat down somewhat. "We'll have to be careful from here on in. I don't know this water. There could be shoals."

Duncan looked ahead with anticipation. It had been cold out there on the water, and he moved about a bit in order to warm up.

On either side, stark stretches of bare rock with occasional patches of stunted black spruce formed a rugged skyline and along the shore were strands of sand interspersed with rocky outcrops. Everything was on a grand scale, and Duncan had great difficulty estimating distances, as there were no obvious points of comparison. Also, even as he looked and looked, he just couldn't see where the river itself actually was. Did it come out between those two low hills to the south, or was that it further over to the west?

"Tide's pretty good," said Charlie. "Been rising for about an hour now. See that line of foam in the water ahead? That's where the tide is meeting the water coming down the river." He then suddenly turned the boat to the south, and for the next five minutes, they followed a diagonal course across the estuary for reasons that Duncan could only guess at. They then turned and did pretty much the same thing in the opposite direction. Charlie grabbed an oar and plunged it into the water. "Four feet," he said.

Overhead, the September sky was a bright cobalt blue with fleecy white clouds which reminded Duncan of sheep in the fields of Aberdeenshire. Increasingly, the rocky hills were clothed in black spruce, with intermittent cliffs of grey rock. On one hillside, however, the trees were so many bare poles, and the precise contours of the land underneath, with its rocks and small cliffs, were laid bare. "What happened there?" Duncan asked, pointing at the spot. Charlie turned to look. "Burnlands," he explained. "A forest fire. Probably started by lightning. Looks like it was maybe two years ago."

He looked out over the water, to left and right, shading his eyes, and then embarked on yet another diagonal.

On the succeeding diagonal, Duncan began to discern a shoal of sand and rocks lying under the water and traversing the estuary. Clearly, one couldn't just take a boat straight up the river. The shoal somehow seemed to be correlated to a feature along the shoreline: a rocky point or a small hill behind.

Presumably, this was something that Charlie instinctively looked for.

The river itself began to reveal itself. Duncan could see where it emerged from the hills to the south. He started to look for a green house with a big deck, for John's house. Charlie saw it first. He saw everything first; it was uncanny. Every time he had seen something and pointed it out to Duncan, it had taken a long while before Duncan could see it himself.

This time was no exception. Perhaps, thought Duncan, it was still the question of scale, of judging distances. Was he looking for a recognisable house, or for a small speck on the horizon? Were those hills as low as they seemed, or were they actually mountains, steep and cluttered with cliffs and deadfalls?

The first thing he noticed was a flagpole with a white, green and blue flag fluttering from the masthead: the Labrador flag.

Then there was the big deck and a sizeable green house behind, on one floor only, with several outbuildings. The house was some fifteen meters above the water's edge, and a mountainside rose steeply behind it. Wooden steps led from the buildings down to the water's edge, where there was a floating dock with a small green canoe lying to one side and an aluminum boat with an outboard tied up to the other.

They were still some five minutes away, but Duncan could see a small woman with grey hair standing on the deck, looking downriver at their boat. That must be John's wife; Melba, she was called.

There was no sign of John.

14

Charlie slowly brought the boat over to the same side of the river as the house, and one could see from the steep riverbanks that here was deep water, and that although there were big rapids just above the house, here there would be little chance of breaking a shear pin or a propellor on an underwater rock. At this point, the river had narrowed, and the current was very strong, even with the rising tide. In the meantime, the woman with the grey hair had been joined on the deck by a young girl, slim and straight, with black hair falling loose to midway down her back.

A sense of excitement came over him as Duncan imagined the moments which were to come. How would John react? How would he look? Would the two of them get on well together?

They tied up at the dock and started up the steps. Duncan made as though to pick up his packsack, but then thought the better of it. He did not wish to appear presumptuous. Ten metres out from the dock, a fat grilse burst out of the water, flashing silver in the afternoon sun. Early on in the summer, the larger salmon came into the river, but as it was now late in the season, the last few stragglers were the smaller salmon, or grilse, of five or six pounds.

Melba met them at the top of the steps, with a smile, yes, but also a question on her face. She knew neither man, although the one with the black moustache at least looked local.

Charlie presented himself. "I'm Charlie Webb, from Postville and Makkovik, and I've brought this here man out to meet his brother."

"Hello," said Duncan in turn. "I'm Duncan Cowan. Does my brother John Cowan live here?"

Melba looked at him as if he was a man from Mars. "You're Jack's brother?" she asked. "Where did you come from?" She quickly corrected herself. "I mean John, of course, but I calls him Jack. And you're his brother?"

"Yes. I'm his younger brother Duncan. And you must be his wife Melba."

"I am. And this is our daughter Sheila," she said, looking very flustered. She ushered the young girl forward. "This is Sheila. Have you come all the way from Makkovik?"

Without waiting for a reply, she added, "Of course you have. And you are looking for Jack. He's upriver, but should be back soon. He's with David. Our son," she added as an afterthought. "Take those oilskins off and come on in to get warm. I have some soup on the stove. A bowl of that will do you no harm, for sure."

They stripped off their rain gear and removed their boots, following Melba into the house. Firstly, there was a screen door, to keep the black flies and mosquitos out, but now there were few flies or mosquitos for it was September.

Then there was the front door itself, and when they passed through it, they were met by a wonderful blast of warm air and the smell of fresh baked bread.

It was a large room, with windows along three sides looking down the estuary, across the river to the further side, and up the river over a big set of rapids that went from one bank to the other. The house was immaculate. Armchairs, a sofa and a low table were placed in front of a big cast-iron stove, with a wooden box beside it full of fire wood. The stove was lit, and the fire made a comforting hiss. Beyond was a dining table, with about ten newly baked loaves of bread standing on racks.

"Sorry for the mess," said Melba, picking up some of the loaves of bread and taking them next door to the kitchen. "It's baking day today. Now I'll get you that soup." Duncan guessed that Melba was happy to retreat to her quarters and gather her thoughts together. She was probably a bit shy and feeling overwhelmed by his sudden appearance.

Never had a bowl of soup tasted better! It was thick with meat and potatoes, plus a few other things. Sheila also produced a loaf of the bread, some knives and plates, and a slab of margarine.

"Pretty good bread," said Charlie to Duncan, helping himself to yet another fat slice. "Your brother is a lucky man."

Duncan was in awe of Charlie's appetite. "That should keep you going for quite a while," he said.

"It may have to," was the reply. Charlie finally stood up, wiped his moustache on his sleeve, and said to Melba, "Missus. I have to go now. I want to reach Makkovik before dark. But this man here would like to stay." Then, turning to Duncan. "Come on down and get your gear. You can keep the oil skins and the boots until you get back to Makkovik."

Duncan stood to one side and fished out two hundred dollars from his wallet. It was probably too much, but better that than too little. He hid the money in his pocket and followed Charlie back down to the boat. It seemed clear that he was invited to stay, although Melba had said nothing. Duncan grabbed his packsack, shook Charlie's hand (all the while slipping him the money), thanked him warmly, and waved farewell to the dead seal.

Back on the deck, the three watched Charlie in silence as

he made his way down the river and out into the open water. In Duncan, the sight called forth that same yearning, that same feeling of space and solitude that he had experienced earlier on in the day. "It must be the Labrador effect," he thought. "Everything up here is so vast, so pristine."

He was sorry to see Charlie go. He had really enjoyed their short friendship. In some obscure way, Charlie reminded him of his uncle Gordon.

Melba broke the silence. "Sheila, you go show our visitor to his room, the one next to David's, and make sure the bed's made up. I'll just tidy up a bit in the kitchen." And to Duncan, "You sir, do you want to wait for Jack here, or would you wish to go upstream to meet him?"

Duncan protested. "Please call me Duncan. I'm John's younger brother. You're my sister-in-law! And yes, Melba, if that's possible, I would like to go to meet him up the river."

Sheila gave him a nod, and he followed her along a short corridor until they reached a door on their right. The walls, the ceiling, the floors: all were in unpainted wood, spruce probably, and of a wonderfully warm colour. On the walls were several marine charts. The bedroom was simple, with two single beds and a wooden chest of drawers. A window looked out onto the hillside which rose behind the house, steep, covered by mosses, dead spruce limbs, and small spruce trees trying to escape the axe and develop their natural height. Duncan deposited his packsack and, noticing a bathroom next to the room, excused himself and went on in to tidy up a bit.

He saw himself in the mirror and reacted with surprise. This was what John would see. Duncan hadn't shaved for two days, and his red hair was matted and unkempt. In particular, he looked quite pale, particularly when he compared his face to the faces now about him. He gave his face a wash and a rub, brushed his teeth and hair, and returned to the living room. Melba was already on the deck, and he went out to join her.

"That's my boat at the dock. It has lots of gas and an

anchor. There's a life jacket in the bottom of the boat; make sure you wear it. Can you handle a boat like that?"

Duncan hesitated, but after all, he had driven Charlie's boat all that morning. "Sure, but where do I go?"

"Take that rattle," she said, pointing at the rapids above the house, "up the middle, avoiding the rocks. When you get near the top, go over to the far side and hug the shore. There's a ledge there, and it's pretty steep, so give it all the gas you can, and once you're over the top, you'll be into the first steady, and you'll find Jack where his boat's at."

Duncan took a deep breath, thanked the lady of the house, went down the steps to the dock, studied the river before him, and tried to imagine himself driving the little boat up those furious rapids. "This is daft," he thought. He looked back at the house, but Melba had already disappeared. "Well, at least, she won't see me making a damn fool of myself."

He put on the life jacket, untied the little boat, lowered the propellor shaft into the water, opened the valve from the gas tank to the fuel line, gave the bulb on it a couple of pumps and started the engine, all as he had seen Charlie do. Switching the boat into reverse, he pulled out from the dock and brought her around. Already, they were being swept downstream, but he switched into forward gear and gunned the motor so that they shot out into the river, heading straight upstream.

He soon found himself in midstream, making steady progress against the current, and doing all he could to keep the boat straight so as not to be turned to one side or the other. Here and there, massive boulders broke the water's surface, and he gave them a wide berth.

Standing up briefly and looking out over the boat's bow, he could now see cliffs closing in on each side and the river narrowing enormously. He cautiously guided the boat over to his left, until he was not far off the further bank, which by now had become a massive cliff with big slabs of granite fractured off lying at the water's edge. He realised that he was not only

looking upstream; he was literally going uphill!

Glancing to his right, he saw deep standing waves ahead and beside him, apparently where the greatest weight of the river was passing through the narrows. He fought to keep the boat straight, gave maximum power, and gradually mounted the wall of water ahead, reaching the smoother water beyond. There was still a terrific current, but now the water was becoming flat, the boat was levelling off and safety lay close ahead. He was entering calmer water, what they apparently called the first steady. He began to relax.

Reducing speed, he examined the river ahead of him. It was once more about three hundred metres wide, and the water was glassy and smooth. There were big boulders here and there along the shores, and what seemed to be a rocky island lay ahead of him. On each side, mountains covered in black spruce rose steeply to a considerable height. Closer to the river was a fringe of alder bushes, with occasionally a little beach at the water's edge.

He passed the island - for that was what it turned out to be - and the river opened up again, revealing a broad panorama of water, alders, stone and sandy beaches and distant mountains. Several hundred metres ahead, on the left-hand shore, there was a spit of sand, and a boat was pulled up in the shallows. "That must be John's," he thought, approaching it steadily.

He beached his boat beside the other one, and looking up, saw a tall figure clad in blue overalls emerging from the alders. He stepped out of the boat on to the sand and pebble beach, and the two brothers stood there, ten metres apart, examining each other without speaking. The constant sound of the river filled Duncan's ears.

"John," he said.

15

"Duncan?" John asked in astonishment, in a deep, melodious voice with the slightest hint of a Scottish accent; or was his in fact a typical Canadian accent?

They remained where they were, neither wishing to make the first move. John was asking himself if this was indeed his brother Duncan. If so, and if he had come all this way to see John, the news had to be bad. Duncan was thinking that he had damn near killed himself coming up the river to greet his long-lost brother, and the bastard didn't even seem to be happy to see him.

"You really are Duncan!" John finally exclaimed. "Well, I'll be damned! Where on earth have you come from?"

Duncan grinned. "Yes. It's me, John. In flesh and blood. I thought I would come out to Labrador just to check up on you!" He walked up the beach towards his brother. John stood there, tall and silent, his face still reflecting his surprise. Duncan was struck by his brother's rugged appearance; this was a mature John, not the tall, awkward brother that he had known thirty years previously.

John took a step or two towards Duncan, but then stopped. "What on earth brings you here? Is everything all right?"

"For sure. Don't worry," Duncan replied. He stopped as well. "You know, you don't look very different from what I expected. Life out here seems to suit you."

John looked at him and smiled. "It depends on what you expected." He examined his brother's face. There were shadows under those eyes, the red hair was now tinged with grey, the jowls seemed a bit full. He tried to recall how Duncan had looked thirty years before, in his army days. "How's Mum?" he asked. "And Sylvia?"

Duncan tried to look reassuring. "The news of Mum and Sylvia is good, even if Mum has had a mild bout of Covid recently and is beginning to get on in years. Mum insisted on my coming out here to see you."

John tried to imagine how they would look, his mother and sister. His mother would certainly be very different from what he remembered. And Sylvia? She would be a grown woman now. "Just to see me?" he asked.

"No. Also to convince you to return home for a visit."

"Why just now?" John asked, seeking to give himself more time to gather his thoughts.

Duncan was getting slightly worried; this was not quite the conversation that he had anticipated. "John," he said. "They would both be really happy to see you. Mum, in particular, talks about you all the time. She sits there in her armchair remembering old stories: John this and John that. She would be over the moon if you would only come back, even just for a flying visit."

"And Mum's Covid?" John asked anxiously. "Is it over now? Is she alright?"

"Absolutely. She only had one or two symptoms. Both Sylvia and I have been visiting her a lot, taking care of her."

"That's good of you. Thank you." John began to feel ashamed of his initial reaction to his brother's sudden appearance. "Duncan," he said. "It's kind of you to come all this way. Mother should be very grateful to you." With that, he stepped forward and gave his brother a strong handshake.

They were interrupted by the arrival of a tall young man with black hair and the beginnings of a moustache carrying a chainsaw and two small tanks of gasoline and chainsaw oil. "Hello," he said. "Who's this Dad?"

"David," said John, "this is your uncle Duncan."

Choosing a long log stranded on the beach up by the alder bushes, the three sat down in the shade and began to exchange their news.

"How do you find it living way up here in the north?" Duncan asked. He was genuinely interested in finding out just what kind of a life his brother led up here in Labrador. "Don't you find yourself isolated?"

John laughed. "Do you know, in fact, this isn't all that far north at all. Check an atlas and you'll see that here, we're actually south of Aberdeen. But to answer your question, I love this land and wouldn't exchange it for anything."

"How can you make a living? Particularly out here on this river?"

"I have one or two properties in Goose Bay that bring in a bit of rent. I also make a few dollars trapping in the winter. That's why David and I are upriver today. We are clearing the trail for my trapping line. It starts here on the river bank and goes up through the alders and then through a bit of spruce forest to the mosses above."

"How long is the trapping line? That must be an enormous job making a trail through all this bush."

"Not really. Once you reach the mosses, the country is pretty open and there's no further need to clear trail. My trapping line is about fifty kilometres long and I travel on a ski-doo with a wooden sled behind. They call the sled a *komatik*."

"You do this in the winter? It must be terribly cold."

"Sometimes. But at the top of the trail, I have a tilt where I can sleep over night."

"What's a tilt?" Duncan asked. He felt as though he was back at school, learning all sorts of new things.

"It's like a small log cabin, six feet square and four feet high, built out of logs with moss stuffed in the cracks and no doors or windows. In the roof there's a trap door. Inside, there's a sort of bed and a little tin stove the size of a shoe box with a chimney made out of Carnation milk tins which sticks out the top of the tilt. You leave a shovel outside, and when you arrive, you shovel all the snow off the roof, go in, light a fire and, soon enough, you're as warm as toast."

At this point, David stirred, and asked, "Dad. Should I bring down the wood we cut?"

"Please do, David," said his father. "Also, don't forget the axe."

"So, tell me," said Duncan, "can we persuade you to make a quick trip back to Scotland?"

"I'll think about it. I would like to see Mum again, that's for sure, and Sylvia as well. But give me a bit of time to think it over and discuss it with Melba. It would be a big decision. And what about you? How is your family?"

Duncan explained his present circumstances, living alone in a big house in Aberdeen, with his wife Ruth and their three children down south in Glasgow. It made him reflect on how unhappy he actually was. This trip to Canada had given him a jolt.

"How long were you in Makkovik?" John then asked.

"Not long at all, at most half a day. Just long enough to meet a man named Charlie Webb, who brought me out here, and a character called Uncle Joe. In fact, these are Uncle Joe's boots. He lent them to me."

David appeared with two six-foot spruce logs on his shoulders and dumped them by the boats, together with an axe. He then returned up the trail. John stood up and stretched. Duncan looked at him and realised how fit he looked. His shoulders and hands seemed particularly broad and strong, undoubtedly from all the manual work which life up here entailed.

"I'll go help," said Duncan, rising in turn. He followed David through the alders and found himself walking up a steep trail through woods of black spruce and the odd stunted birch. What struck him most was the rich forest floor, a soft, spongy carpet of thick moss and lichen.

John appeared behind him and identified the plants for him. "Those low red berries are Canadian dogwood; they have pretty white flowers in summer. The black berries are crowberries, edible, but without much flavour. Those ones there are bakeapples or, if you like, cloudberries; they make excellent jam. All these other bushes with the azalea-like leaves are Labrador tea."

"I see you are still a botanist at heart," Duncan said with a laugh. "What about those red berries that were beside us where we were sitting a moment ago? Are they edible?"

"Those were squash berries. *Viburnum trilobum.* The bears love them, and so do I. While we're at it," John added, "why don't you come on up to the top of the trail and see what the country looks like when you get out of the river valley?"

They went up the steep trail. Gradually, the forest became less thick, and the stunted spruce fewer and fewer. Then they reached a rise of ground, and before them opened up a broad landscape of mosses dotted with the occasional clump of spruce or larch and intersected by any number of little ponds and connecting streams. On the horizon lay a range of dark mountains.

They spotted a caribou over to their left and approached him quietly. He turned out to be a majestic bull, with both antlers fully grown and a fine sleek body. They managed to come within about 30 metres of him before he gave a few grunts and stalked off into a stand of spruce.

"It was fine to come across him like that," John said. "The caribou are more numerous upriver. This is more moose country. But right now, the wolves are giving both populations a very hard time."

Several flights of Canada geese passed close overhead. "Well within shot," said Duncan, who was in the habit of doing a bit of goose shooting back home.

A cold wind was beginning to blow hard out of the east, and there were clouds coming low over the mountain tops that presaged a squall of rain. They headed back to the river, and on their way, picked up more logs. "I assume that this is all for the fire," said Duncan. "That's right," said John. "In the kitchen, we use propane, but I like the smell and companionship of a softwood fire in the living room, and that wood stove can give off a lot of heat."

David was there waiting for them, and for the next ten minutes, he and Duncan carried the remaining logs out of the woods and down to the water's edge, while John stayed on the beach and carefully loaded them into the two boats. "We can't take them all, this time," he said. "I'll fetch the rest tomorrow or maybe, David, you can come up and get them." He then turned to Duncan. "I hope you don't mind if we put a few in your boat. Just be careful and don't go too fast when you get to the narrows."

At this point, the rain that had been threatening arrived, first tentatively and then hard, borne on a driving wind, and they took refuge on their log under the alders. As the three sat there side by side, two otters swam up in the shallows, their bodies sticking straight up out of the water and their heads turning inquisitively, first to one side and then to the other. "Tell me more of mother," said John. "Has it been hard for her, living alone? Is she active out of the house, or in any event, was she before she fell ill?"

The otters had disappeared, but now they could be spotted further upriver, and David rose and walked up the beach to see where they were going.

"She has been very brave, but in some ways, she has had a

difficult time. I think that Dad's death was worse for her than it might otherwise have been because she felt that it was her fault, that she should have done more to stop his drinking."

"It wouldn't have been all that easy," John said. "I remember that Dad was pretty depressed at the end of his life. Farming can be tough. Mum was well out of it when we left Ardeath, even if Gerald Symons did act like a bastard when he terminated the tenancy."

"Yes, and that was also very hard on Mum," Duncan continued. "She felt really guilty about losing the tenancy after Cowans had lived on Bonnycastle for three generations or more."

"Yes, I can imagine." John thoughtfully removed his hat, wiped his hair back off his forehead, and put the hat back on.

"Then you left Scotland after your row with Gerald, and then Gerald's death; that on top of everything else. Mother almost seemed to have been widowed a second time. You were always her favourite, you know."

"I suppose that's true, just as you were closer to Dad."

"Perhaps. When she and Dad were going through that rough patch, it was hard for us not to pick sides."

"Tell me about Sylvia."

"John. I have a confession to make. Sylvia and I haven't been on speaking terms for quite a while. I hardly ever see her nowadays."

"What happened?"

"It was entirely my fault, although it seems to me that Sylvia has been a bit bloody-minded about the whole thing."

"And...?"

"Soon after you left, Sylvia moved out. That was when she was studying accountancy. She shared an apartment with another girl. That's normal enough, but ever since, she has always chosen to live either with another woman or alone."

"But why would this cause you to get on bad terms with her?"

"A while back, I made a snide remark to her. About preferring women to men. Stupid, I know, but that's how it was. Ever since, she refuses to have anything to do with me."

"Yes," John reflected. "That was unwise; you may have touched on a raw nerve end."

"John. I'm afraid I did."

"And where does she live now? Isn't she out at Ardeath?"

"Yes, she is. She has a small cottage on the estate, just near Bonnycastle. This summer, she has become close friends with a woman named Jill Brown, who, according to Mum, is very nice. I believe Jill may even have moved into the cottage with her."

John laughed. "That would make them Syl and Jill! Do you remember, we used to call Sylvia 'Syl'?"

"We still do."

"And what news of the Symons family? Does Keith live out at Ardeath? Does he run the estate?"

"Yes, he does. He is married to a woman named Georgie. They have no children. Keith has never done much else but run the estate, and although I have little to do with him, and certainly don't get up to those parts very often, I understand the big house is in good repair and that the estate appears well-run. It seems that Georgie has a bit of money of her own."

John hesitated. "And Jessica?" he asked at last.

"Do you really want to know?" asked Duncan with a grin.

"Well, yes," said John, feigning indifference.

"Ah, Jessica! To tell you the truth, I have pretty much lost track of her. However, I gather that she is still very beautiful and perhaps a bit wild! She lives somewhere just outside Aberdeen, has gone through several husbands, or men in any event, and apparently owns a flower shop in Aberdeen at the top of Union Street; in fact, not far from the bank where I work, or at least where I used to work."

"Used to work?" John was happy to change the subject.

"Yes. I gave notice just before I left Aberdeen to come out

here."

At this point, the rain stopped, and a warm late afternoon sun appeared through the clouds. The brothers' conversation lapsed, and Duncan rose and stretched.

Their talk had given John much food for thought. He realised with surprise that he was happy to see Duncan once more, to have real contact with his family rather than communication by letter and the odd phone call. He looked forward to hearing more of what Duncan had to tell him. However, it would have to wait until the evening; it was time to head downriver now.

As he sat there alone for a moment more, the image of Jessica flashed through his mind. Those unforgettable times that they had spent together! The old memories came flooding back, wonderful memories, but intermingled with that familiar feeling of remorse as to how he had parted with her thirty years before.

16

Duncan pulled his boat out of the shallows, jumped in, and headed down the river, leaving John on the beach with David. A late afternoon sun shone brightly from the west. He had been up since three that morning, with not too much to eat, and couldn't help feeling that it would be awfully good to have a quick dinner followed by a good night's sleep.

The river began to narrow and ahead of him, Duncan could see the little island just above the rapids. It was a construct of massive boulders precariously heaped one on top of the other, cluttered with the roots of trees and bits of driftwood, and with the odd willow or alder sprouting out of its low spots. Duncan could guess that when the river freed itself of its ice in April or May, the island would be underwater, collecting fallen trees and other debris ripped from the riverbanks upstream, and in turn shifting its boulders about and releasing some of them into the rapids below. "Yes, when the ice goes out," he thought to himself, "this river must be quite a sight."

He passed the island and steered the little boat gently closer to the right-hand shore. Then, for no apparent reason, the outboard engine gave a cough and a splutter, and stopped completely.

Duncan's heart started beating rapidly; he felt weak and the blood rushed to his head. He looked quickly about him and began feverishly to try to restart the engine. It refused. He tried to steer towards the shore, but since the boat had no forward motion, nothing happened. He was being swept down onto the rapids with no hope of avoiding them. The current was taking him away from the shore on his right-hand and down towards those deep standing waves in the middle of the river.

He thought of throwing out the anchor, but it would never hold in that deep, fast water and might only make matters worse.

He looked upstream, and John was nowhere in sight.

Was this going to be the end? Would he end his days drowning in a Labrador river?

The noise of the river increased, and the boat gave a lurch and swung broadside to the current. Duncan had a split second in which to make a decision, to stay with the boat or to jump free of it. His mind suddenly became crystal clear, and his thoughts switched from death to survival.

He jumped.

The water wasn't actually all that cold. At first, he was pulled two or three times under the surface of the water, and each time he swam desperately back up, taking a great gulp of air when he could. Then he remained afloat, thanks in particular to his life jacket, and found himself being swept rapidly downstream. He looked about, and struggled to bring himself closer to the bank, which was still some twenty metres away. Out of the corner of his eye, he saw the boat; it looked strange, and he realised that it was upside down.

He then thought of all the rocks ahead and brought his body around so that he was floating downriver feet first, able to push himself off from any boulder with his feet and to protect his head. After a minute — a crowded, desperate unforgettable minute — he was beyond the worst of it, and although he was still moving fast, he became confident that he was not going to die after all, that life would go on, such as it was.

Ouch! He hit a rock, and just managed to avoid another one, and importantly, to avoid getting caught between the two rocks. That was now the challenge: to make a safe landing, as though he was piloting a plane or a spacecraft!

He was swept over a little ledge, tentatively put his feet down, and felt bottom for the first time. There was no question of his standing up in that current, but by pushing down with his feet, he was able to propel himself towards the bank and relative safety. Finally, the current took him down to a small boulder whose top just broke the water's surface, and here he was able to steady himself and stop himself from being swept further down the river.

The next thing of which he was aware was a woman's voice shouting at him above the noise of the river. "Are you alright?"

Duncan gave a rapid wave of the hand as he clung to his rock.

"Head for that low, flat rock a bit down from you," the voice continued. He was now able to look up.

Duncan couldn't believe his good fortune. There was Melba, not ten feet away from him, kneeling in her little canoe and paddling gently in an eddy over by the shore. He reached the flat rock, gasping and exhausted, and pulled himself on to it.

"Catch your breath a bit," shouted Melba. "Then when you're ready I'll come and get you." Duncan shivered and, sitting up on the rock, emptied his boots one after the other. Looking about, he saw that they were a bit downstream of the house and on the opposite side of the river. He finally beckoned to Melba, and she brought the canoe to the quiet water immediately below his rock. "Hold the bow," she said, "and I'll go to the stern." Duncan obeyed, and then following her directions, got into the canoe, kneeled on its bottom ahead of the bow thwart, and took up a paddle.

"That was a close call," Duncan thought. "I wonder how many men have drowned going down those rapids. And whom am I being rescued by? A woman!"

The little canoe swung out into the river, and they both paddled vigorously on the downstream side. Melba held the canoe at a slight outward angle to the current so that soon, the canoe had ferried across to the further shore, about one hundred metres below the house. Sheila was there on the bank to greet them, slightly out of breath, and caught the bow.

Duncan's legs were so cramped that he nearly collapsed when he got out and stood on the shore.

"Sheila. Take your uncle back to the house; I'll bring up the canoe. And please turn on the generator."

"I already did, Ma."

"Also, could you get him out a big towel so he can take a hot shower?"

"It's waiting for him by the door, Ma."

Duncan and Sheila started along up the side of the river, a shoreline of small boulders and clumps of alder. Finally, they reached the dock, from which the wooden steps took them up to the front of the house. Sheila gave Duncan his towel and discreetly disappeared inside while he peeled off all his wet clothes, leaving them in a soggy heap by the door. He wrapped the towel about his waist and, still shivering slightly, headed for the bathroom and a hot shower. He was alive! And soon, he was warm.

He came to the living room in dry clothes, a new man. Melba was there, anxious to see that he was alright.

"I can't thank you enough, Melba," Duncan said. "I think you saved my life."

"I'm not sure about that," she said, "but I'm sure happy that you're in one piece. Those rapids are pretty rough. You must be a good swimmer."

With a long sigh, Duncan collapsed into a big chair. On the little table in front of the fire was an empty glass, a second glass full of water and a half-empty bottle of single malt whisky. "Help yourself," said Melba. "We've had that bottle for years. A guest once brought it. Jack doesn't touch drink." Duncan helped himself.

John then appeared; he had spoken rapidly to Melba outside. "Thank God you're alive, Duncan," he said. "I'm sorry that had to happen. I really am."

"I hope the boat is alright," said Duncan.

"Oh, don't worry about the boat; David is off fetching it just now."

Pretty soon they were tucking into a dinner of fresh grilse, caught by Sheila that day, with boiled potatoes, greens and bits of deep-fried bread dough, appropriately referred to as sinkers.

"Thanks for coming to get me," Duncan said again to Melba. "How come you arrived so quickly?"

"Sheila came to tell me. She saw you right away. She was down on the dock cleaning her fish."

"That was my last tag," laughed Sheila. Under the catch-and-release rules, a fisherman was only entitled to kill two grilse per season and was required to put a special tag on them as soon as they were caught.

"Like hell it was," said David. "You used up your two tags in June."

There being a pause in the conversation, Duncan rose, asking if he might be excused. He thanked them for the excellent dinner and went gratefully to bed.

17

The next morning, Duncan smelled the bacon from his bed, and then the coffee. He was stiff and his legs ached, and he could quite happily have remained in bed for another hour or two. When he emerged from his room, the others were at the table waiting for him.

"Did you hear a noise last night?" asked John.

"Just the river, but frankly, I was so tired I didn't even hear that."

"There was a black bear outside around ten o'clock, and David went out and fired two shots in the air, just to frighten him away."

"He was right under your window," grinned David. "The bad old bear!" By the general laughter, Duncan concluded that his life had not been threatened, and that bears were an everyday occurrence up there.

After breakfast, John took Duncan out on the deck in front of the house, and they sat together finishing their coffee. "I have been thinking about this trip to Scotland," John started. "I discussed it with Melba. She's dead set against it."

Duncan's heart sank. "Why?"

"She doesn't like it when I'm away. She worries for me.

It's ingrained in her. In the old days, when men went on trips, they often didn't make it back. Not by choice; rather because of the dangers: the sea, the ice, the polar bears. That sort of thing."

"But you? Shouldn't you come all the same? Don't you feel that you owe it to Mother? If you refused after all this, after my coming out here to look for you, she would be devastated."

John flushed in anger. "Don't pressure me, Duncan. I understand all that."

"I'm not trying to pressure you, John. I am just stating the obvious."

John felt trapped. Duncan was right. "Give me a bit of time," he said. "I'll speak to Melba again."

They then started to recall their old times together. "Do you remember," said Duncan, "when you and I got that summer job down in Newburgh cleaning boats?"

John laughed. "Oh yes! How could I forget? Mr Chalmers' boatyard. It gave us a bit of pocket money."

"I'll always remember our lying on our backs under the hulls scraping and sanding. Old Chalmers would come around from time to time to make sure we weren't loafing, and you would rub two pieces of sandpaper together just to make a convincing noise."

John laughed. "Then there was the time," he said, "when you got into trouble with that girl in Ellon and Dad had to fix things up with her parents."

"She was fun," said Duncan. "I should have stayed with her longer." He gave his brother a sly look. "Like you did with Jessica."

"That was different..." John began to say, but then he decided it was best not to continue.

They talked on for the rest of the morning, chatting idly and enjoying the view out across the river to the mountains beyond.

That afternoon, after talking once more with Melba,

John announced that he was going to return with Duncan for a three-weeks' visit to Scotland, and they all sat around in the living room discussing details. Melba didn't wish to remain alone on the river for that long and decided that she and Sheila would go to stay with Melba's sister in Makkovik, where, in any event, Sheila was to start school in less than a week's time.

"So, you go to school in Makkovik," Duncan said to Sheila. "Is it a good school? I met a man on the ferry named Bill Kane. Is he one of your teachers?"

"Mr Kane! Sure he is. He teaches history, mathematics and chemistry. He also runs our little orchestra." She hesitated. "Really, it's more like a band. We play mostly simple music, but sometimes classical as well."

"What instrument do you play?"

"She plays the fiddle," David said. "Play us something, Sheila. Play us *Hey Johnnie Cope*."

She laughed and made an attempt at a Scottish accent. "Hey Johnnie Cope, are ye wauking yet!" Turning to her uncle, she added, "You'll think you're back in Scotland already." David fetched her fiddle. She stood apart, put it under her chin, tuned it a bit, and played *Johnnie Cope*.

Duncan had to fight hard to keep the tears from his eyes.

John noticed this and said to his brother, "Don't worry, Duncan. One of Canada's greatest authors, Hugh MacLennan, wrote that to be a Scot is never to be far from tears."

During the day, Duncan looked around outside. A path led to a hut in the woods where oil drums and a generator were kept. Behind the house was a root cellar. Coming from a spring up the hillside was a pipe carrying drinking water. Skids led from the dock up the hill so that the dock could be winched up the hill for the winter, out of danger from the ice. Everything was in perfect order.

He also explored the house a bit more, and in particular noticed all the bookshelves on the non-window side of the living room. They were filled and more: reference books, children's books, a lot of fiction. A few were in French.

John took the weather forecast and informed them that he would go to Makkovik the next day with Duncan, Melba, and Sheila. They were to be ready to leave by six in the morning. David was to remain behind to start closing up the house.

That night, they had a very acceptable stew of moose meat, and lingered long at the table as Duncan told them stories of Scotland. John brought up the subject of the US president and asked Duncan whether he thought he would be re-elected.

"What a dummy!" interjected Sheila. "He grabs women between the legs."

"Sheila!" exclaimed Melba, looking mortified.

"It's true, Ma. It's true. You just don't keep up with the news."

Before turning in, they went out onto the deck to admire the night sky. Overhead was the polar star. Then, as if on cue, they were treated to a wonderful display of northern lights playing across the entire sky. They were a milky white and made the open sky behind look a pale, intense aubergine. The patterns shifted constantly, blocking out the stars behind.

Melba spoke thoughtfully. "My mother used to say that if you whistled to the northern lights, they would tickle you and make you dance. 'Don't you go whistling to the northern lights,' she would say to us, 'or they'll surely tickle you.'" She felt somehow that those northern lights were a bad omen for the trip that John was going to take, but didn't say so.

The next morning was mild, and there was neither fog nor wind. They left sharp at six. David saw them off at the dock and gave his mother and sister big hugs. Duncan felt of two minds about leaving so quickly; he had already developed a taste for this land, for the long, ragged sky-lines of black spruce and the constant rumour of the river. He resolved to return one day if he possibly could.

Going out into the estuary of the Big River was magic. To the east, the morning sun rose above clouds stretching orange and pink across the horizon, whilst below, the waves danced dark blue and pink, with what seemed to be ripples of fire in them. Up and down the coast, the rough cliffs, bald mountains and rocky islands were drowned in a brilliant light.

The trip was uneventful, and they reached Makkovik in the middle of the afternoon. There they discovered that there was a Twin Otter flight scheduled for the next morning from Makkovik to Goose Bay. John and Duncan made reservations and purchased their tickets.

The next morning, they all drove out to the little landing strip together. Melba's face was impassive. If she felt unhappy or anxious, she didn't show it. On the other hand, John was nervous and a bit testy; he didn't know why exactly, but he felt apprehensive about his imminent trip to Scotland.

18

Jill was beginning to think seriously about writing her next article on the circumstances surrounding Gerald Symons' death. She felt that there might be something there, something that she could get her teeth into. She summarised the facts to herself as she knew them.

At the time of his death, Gerald was married, in his fifties, and living with his wife and two children in Ardeath House. He was important locally; he was the laird of Ardeath. He liked to shoot. He had an apparently beautiful young daughter, Jessica, who was having an affair with John Cowan, a son of one of his agricultural tenants. He tried to stop Jessica from seeing John. He evicted the Cowans as tenants and hard feelings arose between them. He and John Cowan even had a fistfight in the dining room of the big house, and Gerald was worsted. And finally, one October afternoon, Gerald went out shooting alone and was found dead from a blast of his own gun. John was somewhere out on the estate seeing Jessica at the time. After Gerald's death, Ardeath was inherited by his son Keith.

"Where do I start?" Jill asked herself. "And what am I looking for?" Both were good questions. There was one obvious challenge: the whole affair had taken place some thirty years previously.

Jill first quizzed Sylvia. "Tell me, Syl, what is there that might be helpful and that I don't already know?"

Sylvia frowned. "About the day he died? I have told you everything I can."

"What about Gerald's friends, his family?"

"I'm sorry Jill. I was only nineteen at the time. I barely knew the man."

"Were he and his wife happy?" Jill asked. "Did you ever hear that they were not getting along well together?"

"How would I have known?" Sylvia reflected for a moment. "There was one thing a bit unusual, I suppose."

Jill looked up. "What was that?"

"I think that perhaps Gerald kept a mistress on the estate. There is a red brick house a little beyond the main drive that leads up to the big house. Behind a tall hedge. You may have noticed it. We used to joke about it. We called it the love house. A woman called Margaret Downie lived there." Sylvia was searching back in her memory. She wanted to be helpful.

Jill prodded her. "What makes you think she was Gerald's mistress?"

"It was a rumour - nothing more. We may have been imagining things. It was just that we often saw Gerald walking over there, on that part of the estate, and sometimes going through the gate leading to Margaret's house. When I think of it, Gerald wasn't in the habit of visiting his tenants. He had a factor do that for him. So, any visits he may have made with Margaret would have been unusual."

"Do you remember anything about her? Her age? Her appearance?"

"We barely ever saw her. I think she would have been in her late twenties, and as I recall, not bad looking."

That was all that Jill could learn from Sylvia, but it gave her one possible lead.

That morning, Jill had actually met Keith Symons. He had come around to the cottage looking to collect some money from Sylvia. The encounter had been brief, but she could tell that Keith was hard, haughty, and not an immediately promising source of information. In any event, she thought it wiser to tap some peripheral sources first before talking to such obvious targets as Keith.

Incredibly, she had also talked with Jessica Symons on the phone. An unexpected reward for having the idea that she and Syl should send Mary some flowers. But pursuing that lead could wait as well.

The first thing that she did do was to search the Internet for contemporary newspaper accounts. There was barely any information on Gerald's death itself. The family was said to be in shock and Keith was identified as successor to the estate. She succeeded in finding the name of the police officer who announced the results of the enquiry, concluding that Gerald had died from the accidental discharge of his gun. However, she then found that the officer had retired shortly after and died in the course of the next few years.

A search for Margaret Downie yielded no results.

She had more luck with the identity of Gerald's widow. She proved to be a woman named Andrea Quinn, born in the Irish Republic. She was now an artist and occasionally exhibited her works locally. Jill picked up the phone and called at work.

"Hi, Sarah. It's Jill." Sarah was one of Jill's colleagues at the Post Office. "Do you have a moment?"

"For sure, Jill. What is it?"

"Can you find me the address and telephone number of a woman named Andrea Quinn?"

"Easy," was the answer. "Hang on. Won't be long. Yes. Here she is. Have you a pencil and paper?"

"Yes. Fire away." Sarah read out the details. Jill thanked her and rang off.

Jill then decided to go down to the local pub. There, as she had hoped, were Jock and Sandy sitting quietly in a corner. "Do you mind if I join you?" she asked once she had a glass of lager in her hand.

The two men were both surprised and delighted. "For sure," said Sandy, waving his hand towards an empty chair. "Our pleasure."

They chatted for a while, and Jill was able gradually to lead the conversation to the subject of Sandy's job as keeper on Ardeath estate. "How long have you been keepering at Ardeath?" she asked him.

Sandy thought for a while. "Going on twenty-eight years," he said proudly, "and I was underkeeper for Mr Gerald before."

"Keith's father," said Jill. "What like of man was he?"

"Oh, a fine man, wouldn't you say Jock?" The other nodded. "And a great shot. One of the best in the country."

"Is Keith a good shot as well? Is he like his father was?"

Sandy hesitated. "I wouldn't wish to say a bad word about either man, but I will say this. The father was the better shot." Jill sensed that Sandy was beginning to wonder why she was so interested in the subject. Possibly he was torn between a loyalty to his employer and a personal view that he might have wished to express.

"Was he in good health when he died?"

"In top form. Mr Gerald was always walking ahead of everyone else. He never stopped. And he was popular, too. He had a lot of friends."

"It must have been a bit of a shock when..." Her voice trailed off.

"It was terrible! Such a fine man. Dying like that."

"Are accidents like that common up here? Shooting accidents, I mean."

"Never! Well, there is the odd youngster that shoots himself in the foot. Older men usually stop shooting before they are unsteady. But an experienced shot when he's still going strong. Accidents like that..."

"Bad luck," said Jill.

"Yes ma'am. Just bad luck."

Jock, who had been following the conversation in silence, looked down at his glass and added his agreement. "Och aye," he said. "Bloody bad luck."

Jill finished her glass and took her leave. She always enjoyed chatting with people like Sandy and Jock. In addition, however, this conversation tended to strengthen her conviction that whatever else it had been, Gerald Symons' death was not accidental.

When she arrived at the cottage, Sylvia had just returned from seeing her mother in Aberdeen.

"Hi, Syl. I bought your mum those flowers."

"Good going. How much do I owe you?"

"It was forty pounds in all, so you owe me twenty. I bought them from a florist who turned out to be Jessica Symons. She asked after you."

"No!" Sylvia exclaimed. "Jessica? That's incredible. You can tell me more about it later. Meanwhile, I have great news. John has agreed to come home. He and Duncan called Mum from Saint John's late last night. Duncan expects to arrive in Aberdeen tomorrow. John needs a couple of days to sort out his passport and should get here on Friday." Her eyes were sparkling. "Can you imagine? Thirty years will have gone by, seeing John again after thirty years. It's incredible." She wrapped her arms around Jill. "He's the only man I ever trusted."

19

"I hear that John Cowan may be coming back to Scotland for a visit," said Georgina Symons to her husband Keith as they sat having tea in the library of Ardeath House.

Keith hated it when his wife disturbed him while he was reading his newspaper, but this time it was different. "What?" he asked. "Say that again. What did you hear?"

"It's just a rumour, but a reliable one. The cleaning lady told me. Duncan Cowan went out to Canada on a flying visit to look for his brother John. The family was hoping that Duncan would convince John to come back to Scotland for a visit. It seems he may have succeeded." Georgie was enjoying herself. It was not often that she could tell her husband about what was going on. Usually, it was the opposite.

Keith looked extremely unhappy. "It would be better for all of us if John remained in Canada."

Keith Symons was a big man and strongly built for his fifty-odd years. He was bald and wore a moustache. He was short-tempered, bigoted, and lacked charm. He was also slightly deaf. However, he was the laird, the proprietor of Ardeath estate and master of Ardeath House. In succession to his father Gerald.

The house itself was Victorian in age and design. It had been built at the time of Keith's great grandfather, who had made a lot of money in the coal business. It counted a drawing room, a dining room, a library, a billiard room, an estate office, the kitchen of course, and numerous bedrooms. It had central heating and modern plumbing. It was very large for just two inhabitants.

The library where they sat was a long narrow room, the walls lined with books on two walls, at one point framing a door leading out into the central passage of the house. There was a fireplace set in the middle of the third wall between two windows, and the view on that side was of lawn and large clumps of rhododendrons. On the fourth wall was a door leading out into a conservatory.

Various paintings hung on the walls as space permitted. There was a depiction of the battle of Blenheim, showing Marlborough urging his troops across a little bridge. There was also an old map of Australia showing the places where the first colonists were settled. A comfortable, if worn, settee occupied the centre of the room in front of the fire, which was burning lazily. The floors were generously covered with a variety of oriental carpets.

Georgie sat there knitting. She was of roughly the same age as Keith, but somehow seemed ageless. Her dark hair was tied up in a bun and she wore a brown wool skirt and a red cardigan. She was on the plump side and spoke English with traces of a Dutch accent, as she originally came from Utrecht in the Netherlands. Her parents had moved to London when she was in her teens.

"What's that you're knitting?" Keith asked his wife, somewhat impatiently. He felt that his wife knitted too much and neglected the housework.

"Socks for the nieces." She and Keith had no children of their own, and that was a great shame she felt, because what would happen to the estate after they were gone? She counted her stitches carefully and then put her knitting aside. "Why would you be upset if John Cowan came back for a visit?"

Keith didn't answer. It was none of his wife's business. However, she was right: he would be upset. "John had better stay off the estate," he said to himself.

"Why do you think he's coming?" Georgie persisted. "Do you think that he'll get in touch with your sister?"

"He can do whatever he bloody well likes," Keith replied impatiently. At the present time, there was no love lost between Keith and his sister Jessica. He couldn't even remember the last time he had seen her. "When John and Jessica started going out," he stated, "Jessica was only sixteen. Far too young. I told her that she was making a fool of herself, but she had a fit and told me to mind my own business. I was only trying to be helpful, but she's like that."

"What about the rest of your family?" Georgie asked. "Wasn't your father opposed to her seeing John?"

"That's putting it mildly. He was furious."

"Do you think that that's why your father and John had that famous fight in the dining room?"

"I'm sure that's why. I bet Dad didn't have a chance. Probably John took him by surprise." Keith had always felt humiliated by the outcome of that fight: his father flat on the dining room floor with a bloody nose, and his Mother and Jessica ushering John out of the house as fast as they could. Keith himself had been somewhere else at the time; he liked to think that had he been present, he would have repaid John in kind.

Georgie was wearying of life in Aberdeenshire. The pandemic had only made matters worse. No bridge with their neighbours, the Nortons. No outings to buy woolens in Elgin. No visitors from the south. No dinner parties to organise. Just day after day in that enormous house with Keith. True, it would probably be no better at this time down south. However, there at least, or so it seemed to her, there was less wind, less cold and less mud.

Yes, the wretched mud; you couldn't take three steps outside without walking in it, or worse. This was a man's world. The men could go out, dressed in their barbours and wellingtons, and shoot pheasant, repair fences, deliver calves and harvest barley, but what was there for a woman to do? "Knit," she grumbled.

She put her knitting down and took a sip of her tea. "All in all, it was better for us all that John left, and that he did so so soon after your father's death. Imagine, otherwise we might have had him as an in-law."

Keith mumbled something under his breath.

"I sometimes wonder about your father's death," Georgie continued after picking up her knitting again. "There was a lot of talk at the time, wasn't there?"

"What talk?" Keith looked up rather sharply.

"I don't know. I wasn't around. But I heard later that there had been talk, speculation about the circumstances surrounding your father's death."

"Georgie, I don't know what you're getting at. All I can say is that my father's death was an accident, that he stumbled, fell, and shot himself. Mother was with me when we found him, and that's how it looked. The police came and that's what they concluded."

"I was once told that John and Jessica were together at the time, somewhere nearby on the estate," Georgie said. "Is that so?"

"Apparently," Keith replied.

"Perhaps they saw something. Perhaps even John had something to do with what happened."

Keith looked angry. "Georgie. Come on! Perhaps this. Perhaps that. We are going back almost thirty years and I fail to see the advantage of stirring the pot."

Keith checked his watch. "I have to go out and see Mitchell in twenty minutes." He was referring to Sandy Mitchell, the estate's gamekeeper, who was in the final stages of organising that season's pheasant shooting.

Keith rose from his big armchair and put two logs on the fire. The logs were very short, as the fireplace was a converted coal grate. Before sitting down again, he looked along the lines of books burdening the old mahogany bookshelves. They were old books, dating at least back to the Great War. Here and there were gaps where the exigencies of the estate's finances had caused Keith to call on the local antique dealer.

He turned to Georgie: "How are your finances? Could you lend me five thousand until October? The shooting syndicate's second payment is due on the third, when we hold the first shoot."

"But Keith! That's not fair. I lent you two thousand three weeks ago. Where does it all go?"

"It was more than three weeks ago, and you can't imagine what it costs to run this estate. It all adds up."

"But the estate has revenues. Surely they must be enough to cover all that?" Georgie had very little knowledge of the estate's finances, except to know that she was constantly encroaching on her family money in order to subsidise them.

"They would if I could only get our rents up to market rates and collect outstanding bills. But the tenants are impossible. This morning, I went around to collect an amount from Sylvia Cowan. She wasn't there, and I had to deal with a little Glaswegian woman who is staying with her. I came away empty-handed. Georgie," he finished. "Money just doesn't grow on trees."

Keith left the room. "John," he was thinking, "that bastard. He had better stay away from around here."

20

Jill reflected the next morning on her chat with Sandy. He had confirmed her suspicion that experienced shots like Gerald Symons didn't often have shooting accidents, particularly fatal ones. She needed to know more about events on that day long ago.

It just so happened that she also wanted to find a present for Sylvia, whose birthday was coming soon. In the window of the antique shop in Ellon, by the Post Office, there was a small acrylic painting, a landscape, which she had come to admire. It suddenly struck her that it was signed *A Quinn*. They had to be the same person: Gerald's widow, Andrea Quinn, and the artist whose little landscape she so liked.

Jill gave it some thought. She decided she would first buy a painting for Sylvia, striking up a relationship with the artist, and later, go back and ask the questions that she was so eager to have the answers to. This was Jill's way of doing things. She was very methodical.

That afternoon, she hopped into her Mini and set out for Aberdeen. She found the address without difficulty, parked nearby, and went to have a look. There was a small house with a sign at the street saying *A. Quinn, Landscape Artist*, then a little gate and an open garage door. The garage held no car; it was the artist's studio. On the walls were numerous small paintings in her style, a large shelf with pots full of brushes and bottles of matte medium, gesso and varnish, a wall clock and a crucifix.

"Hello," Jill said to the slim elderly lady who was sitting at a table working on a sketch. "Am I disturbing you?"

"Of course not," said the other with a smile. "Please fetch yourself that chair. You can set it down right there where you are standing. Do have a seat. I'm delighted to have a bit of company."

Jill looked at her. "She must have been very pretty in her day," she thought. "Fair hair, a lovely long neck, graceful hands." She brought the chair over and sat down.

"I work in Ellon and have been admiring a little painting of a church that hangs in the antique shop window. I think it is one of yours."

The artist smiled. "Possibly. I don't recall which one it might be, but yes, I have sold the odd painting in Ellon and thereabouts."

Out of the corner of her eye, Jill had started to glance at the paintings hanging on the walls of the garage. They were all very attractive, she found. "Have you painted all your life?"

"Not really. I took it up some time ago when my husband died. I have always enjoyed art though, and painting is now what I live for. It's very absorbing and permits you to discover a little about yourself as well."

"That's interesting. In what way?"

"Well, as you go through life, you have a number of experiences. In a sense, you are the sum total of these experiences. When you paint, little bits of you find their way into the painting you are working on. Your secret thoughts and hidden reminiscences."

Jill nodded with a smile. "In that painting in Ellon, you almost have to guess that it's a church. What I particularly like are the colours that swirl about. Now that I think about it, they are colours that seem to be suggestive of stained-glass windows."

"Do you ever paint yourself?" The artist put away her sketch book and crayons. She felt that she had finished for the day.

"No, but I love textiles. I used to work in a clothes shop in Glasgow and what drew me to it were the colours, the patterns and the textures of the cloth which I was handling."

The artist nodded. "Please go and have a look around. You can have any of the paintings which you see behind me on the walls. They are all the same price: two hundred pounds."

"That doesn't seem very much."

"I get by. At my age, you spend very little. Also, I would be happy to think that one of my paintings was hanging in your home, an orphan finally adopted!" They both smiled at the metaphor.

"Quinn is an Irish name, I think. Do you originally come from Ireland?"

"Yes. My family is from Limerick. I have lived up here most of my life, though. Ever since I was married."

Jill rose to look over the paintings inside the garage. She had already made her choice, but there were quite a few others that could have tempted her. There were fishing boats, upended so their hulls could be cleaned; castles in various states of ruin; harbours with waves breaking angrily over the breakwater; dunes of bent grass, leaning away from the wind. "May I take this one?" she asked, removing her choice from the wall. "It's to give as a birthday present. To the woman I live with."

"With pleasure. That's the square and pond in the village near where I used to live. Quite close to Ellon, in fact."

"Yes. I recognised it at once. My friend and I know that spot well. We live on Ardeath estate, close by." The artist gave Jill a curious look but said nothing. Jill handed her two hundred pounds and the artist carefully wrapped the painting in a sheet of brown paper. "I have taken a lot of your time and must now be on my way," Jill said. "It has been a great pleasure meeting you."

"As it has been for me. I hope that you will come back another time."

"I would like that. I really would. My name's Jill, by the way."

"And mine's Andrea."

21

As Duncan's plane circled above London Heathrow, he had plenty to think about. He was truly proud to think that he had succeeded in his mission to convince John. "Mum was so happy when we called to tell her!" he thought. "She sounded as though she was close to tears. I suppose she told Sylvia right away." The sudden thought of his sister brought a sinking feeling to his stomach and robbed him of some of his satisfaction. He really had to find a way of making amends.

What were his own plans for the future, now that he had given notice to the bank? The trip had given him a new perspective, had caused him to think more positively about himself and about the choices that lay before him.

He had truly enjoyed his exposure to Labrador, but the idea of actually living there didn't appeal to him. It was just too isolated, too new. For John, it had been a different matter; he had taken the plunge at twenty-five. Duncan was now in his fifties, and that was not an age for such a radical departure.

His best bet was to follow up on the idea of buying his uncle Gordon's interest in the *Sunset Sea*, and operating the trawler jointly with Gordon's two sons, Bill and Jim.

He wondered if the bank had found someone to fill his

position. There were one or two sensitive files that he had been dealing with at the time of his departure. One involved a series of substantial transactions with a bank in one of the Baltic states. As the bank's compliance officer, it had been his responsibility to ensure that the transactions were legal. For that reason, he had been doing enhanced due diligence on the Baltic bank. Another involved loans requested of the bank by a developer who seemed to be losing money hand over fist, so that you wondered if there wasn't another motive for his operations, such as money laundering. There were also a few run-of-the-mill cases of potential tax evasion involving offshore companies and trusts. Yes. His successor would be busy, and the bank would have to act quickly to fill the position.

The plane landed at Heathrow and Duncan had no problem making the connection to Aberdeen, as he had kept his packsack with him.

It felt somehow as though he had been away for years. The contrast between Heathrow and the landing strip at Makkovik defied description! On the other hand, when his plane started circling overhead Aberdeen, the feeling was the opposite: it was as though he had never been away.

He looked out the window of the plane. There was the River Dee, winding down from the west and shining in the morning sun, and there, the Hill of Fare and Banchory. He had a glimpse of small fields surrounded by stone walls, of sheep scattered everywhere. They flew a tight circle low over the River Don. He was home!

From the airport, he took a taxi to his house. After a hot shower and a change of clothes, he called his mother.

She answered after the first ring. "Duncan! Welcome back. Are you tired? When are you going to come over? Have you photos? What does John look like? Has he changed? When does he get here?" She was in a state of great excitement and kept asking her questions without waiting for the answers.

"Of course John has changed, Mum. Haven't we all? He

is tall, strong but slim, no moustache or beard. His hair is still dark brown. He dresses simply, and he has a deep voice, just as he used to have."

"What is his wife like?"

"Melba? I think that you would like her very much. She is a bit younger than John, I think. When you look hard, you can see that she has a bit of Inuit in her, but clearly, all along the Labrador coast, almost everyone is in some degree a mixture of European and Inuit. She is on the short side and a bit stout, is a great cook and keeps a very tidy house."

"Tell me about the children."

"They're charming. You would love them. Tomorrow, I'll show you some photos. The oldest, David, must now be sixteen or seventeen. He is very competent, very mature; tall, strong, and handsome, as they say. The girl, Sheila, looks a bit more Inuit than does David. She would be about fourteen. She is very bright and independent, and good-looking in her own way. She plays the fiddle like an angel."

"What about their house?"

"It's in a stunning location, all by itself on that very large river, and it is very comfortable. I do wonder, however, what it's like there in the wintertime. They are by the sea, so in a way, the cold is perhaps not as severe as you might expect, but they apparently get vast amounts of snow."

The conversation could have gone on for hours, but Duncan was tired, so he asked his mother to forgive him and promised to bring her the photos the next day.

Checking his telephone messages, he found that he was urgently requested to contact a woman named Joan McIntosh at the bank, and also his wife Ruth. Neither message filled his heart with joy, and he decided he deserved a good rest, and that Joan and Ruth would just have to wait until the morrow.

He felt fine the next morning and, coffee in hand, called Ruth down in Glasgow.

"Where have you been?" she demanded. "I called you last

week."

"In Labrador," he answered as casually as he could. There was a long silence.

"In Labrador?"

"Yes. In Labrador."

"Duncan, joking apart, I need to talk to you. Urgently. It's about the children."

"What about the children?"

"Well, it's not really about the children. It's about us. Duncan, I want a divorce."

Duncan groaned inwardly, but was not surprised. The likelihood of a divorce had been hanging in the air for some time now. "Ruth. I'm only just back from a long trip. Please give me a week or two to sort a few other things out, then we can meet and discuss it. OK?"

"If you say so, but I'm dead serious."

"I understand."

The next call was to the bank. Sue, the receptionist, answered his call with competence and warmth. "Duncan! How are you? We miss you already. What can I do for you?"

"Hi, Sue. Good to hear your voice. I'm returning a call from Joan McIntosh."

"Oh!" From Sue's voice, Duncan inferred that Ms McIntosh had already made an impact at the bank. "One minute. I'll see if I can locate her."

"Good morning. Joan here," was the next thing Duncan heard.

"Hello, this is Duncan Cowan returning your call. Apologies for the delay, but I've been out of the country."

"Thank you, Mr Cowan. Excuse me for a moment while I return to my desk." There was a pause. " Yes, here we are. I am the one who is replacing you in Compliance, at least temporarily. The bank has transferred me up from Edinburgh, where I usually work."

"Is there something that I can help you with?" Duncan

asked.

"No longer, thanks. I did have some questions, but I was able to find all the answers. Since we're on the line, however, perhaps I should tell you that I have referred one or two of the files involving offshore bank accounts to the Inland Revenue. Apart from that, if I need to talk to you again, I hope that you won't mind if I call you."

"No problem," said Duncan, and rung off. Absentmindedly, he wondered which files had been referred to the tax authorities. Would one of them be Georgina Symons?

22

Jill returned from her visit with Andrea with the painting on the back seat of her car in its wrapping of brown paper. Sylvia was already there, and Jill, unable to wait, presented her with the package. "Happy Birthday, Syl, a day or two in advance."

"Jill! You're wonderful! For my birthday! How did you find out?" Sylvia was really happy and gave Jill a big hug. "You didn't have to give me anything. Just our being together is all I want!"

She eagerly unwrapped the parcel and held the painting up for inspection. "It's super! I see - it's the little park in the village." She examined the artist's signature. "Who is A. Quinn? Is she someone from around here?"

"You are going to have a bit of a surprise. She is Andrea Symons. Quinn is her unmarried name."

"Andrea Symons!" Sylvia took another look at the painting. "She's very good. I like it, I really do. Thanks a lot, Jill. How did you ever end up buying a painting from Andrea Symons?"

"What happened is that there is a painting that I recently noticed and liked, hanging in the antique shop in Ellon. I asked in the shop, found out the artist's name, and realised that she was the same person as Gerald's widow. I was able to kill two birds with one stone: buy you a present and meet Gerald's widow. She was very friendly and we got along very well together."

"Did you ask her any questions about Gerald's death?"

"No. I decided that it would be better to go back to see her for a second visit. That way, she might be a little more inclined to tell me what happened." Sylvia was examining the painting. "Don't lie to me; if you don't like it, I can always take it back."

"Absolutely not. I like it very much. Let's hang it here." Sylvia went to fetch a hammer and a hook and nail, and within a minute, the painting was in a place of honour beside the fireplace.

"Incidentally," Sylvia said, "I had a call earlier on from Jock; for some reason or other, he would like to talk to you. He said that if you wanted to go down to the village tomorrow at about eleven, you would find him beside the little pond."

Jill looked up. "He wanted to talk to me. Did he say about what?"

"No. Just that he wanted to see you."

"That's very interesting. He was there when I had my little chat with Sandy. Hopefully he wants to add something."

The next morning, Jill was off to the village at a quarter to eleven. Jock was installed on a bench near the pond, a fat black Labrador lying at his feet on a leash. Jill sat down beside them. "Good morning, Jock. How are you?"

"Good morning," he replied. Giving a sharp tug on the leash, he ordered his dog to stay quiet.

"Was she a good working dog in her day?" Jill enquired.

"Aye, she was," said Jock. "Mostly for the ducks. She could hear them coming. I just had to watch her." He chatted on for a while about duck shooting up on the mosses and about his days as water bailiff on the Ythan.

"Why did you want to speak to me?" Jill finally asked. "Did it have something to do with Gerald Symons?"

Jock looked at her. He nodded affirmatively, waiting for her to ask another question.

"Did you know Gerald Symons well?" Jill asked.

"Oh aye. I met him fishing quite often. And shooting. Also, as a tenant. I was many years a tenant on Ardeath estate; I only moved into the village about three years ago."

"What was he like?"

"A tall man and thin; strongly built. He was quiet, though, and kept his own counsel."

Jill thought a bit. "Did you notice any changes in him in his last years?"

"Not really." Jock hesitated. "Do you mean over the years, or just before the end?"

"Just before the end."

"I would say yes. He seemed to me to be an unhappy man at the end. A worried man. I can't say why I felt that; it was just the way he looked, I guess."

"Do you think his marriage was a happy one?" Jill asked.

"I don't know anything about that."

"Do you remember a woman named Margaret Downie?"

"Who doesn't?" Jock's face lit up with a faint smile. "She had a bit of a reputation. Good looking, but it was said that she was very free with her favours."

"How long did she live on the estate?"

He thought for a while. "Six or eight years, I would say."

"Did she and Gerald seem close?"

"I should think they were. He visited her in her house pretty often."

By now, Jill had concluded that Margaret had almost certainly been Gerald's mistress, and that he had set her up in a house on the estate so as to have her close at hand. At the same time, she was beginning to suspect that there might have been more to it than that.

"Do you know if she had a job somewhere? Did she go out often? Did she go into the village to shop?"

Jock spoke thoughtfully. "No, we didn't see much of her in the village. What was unusual was that she sometimes went away for short trips. I don't know where. A car would come to fetch her, and off she would go. I knew because my cottage was just next to her house. I sometimes saw her drive by."

"In a car with a driver? That's strange."

"Yes, I thought so."

"Was it always the same car? Do you know who the driver was?"

"Yes, always the same car. A taxi, from New Deer. I don't know who the driver was, except that it was a woman."

"How old would Margaret have been at the time Gerald died?"

"Not very old. Perhaps thirty." Just then a pigeon alighted on the edge of the pond and Jock's dog attempted a dash at her. Jock had the leash in his hand, however, and brought her up short. "Fit ye deen, lassie," he cried at her. The dog sat down again and looked lovingly up at him. "These working dogs are very affectionate," Jill thought to herself, "and also long-suffering."

She had a further question for Jock. "You said earlier that at the end, Gerald was an unhappy man. Do you think that Margaret Downie had anything to do with it?"

"Yes," was the simple answer.

"Why?" Jill looked expectantly at Jock.

He didn't disappoint her. "About two or three days before Mr Gerald died, I saw them drive by in his car. They were hard at it."

"Arguing, you mean?" He nodded. "I wonder if Margaret Downie is alive today," she continued.

"I don't know. She left shortly after Mr Gerald died and hasn't been seen around here ever since."

23

John ducked his head as he exited the plane and went cautiously down the ramp. He looked about. Aberdeen airport had certainly changed over the last thirty years!

He was nervous. He feared that he would find his mother and sister changed, that they would be as strangers, that he would not be able to share the same bond with them as in days gone by.

He also felt guilty about having left Scotland in the way he had, without much warning or explanation. He was not even certain in his own mind which explanation he would have given. Would he have said that he wanted to make a new life for himself or that he wanted to make a break with Jessica? Or what?

Could there have been a more abstract reason, an impatience with rural Scotland's class differences, with the suspicion that from the day you were born, your future was there for you to live, detailed and immutable?

He entered the terminal building.

He wasn't expecting to be met but looked around at all the faces, just in case. Suddenly, he saw Sylvia. "Hello, stranger!" she was shouting, waving both arms in great excitement.

"Sylvia! How wonderful!" They shared a long embrace.

"Wow!" she said. "You've nearly crushed the breath out of me! Life in Canada must agree with you." John seemed very fit, very strong; his face was weather-beaten, but fresh. Sylvia was ecstatic. Her big brother was home! She was proud to stand beside him. She wondered how he would find Aberdeen after all these years. Would he and his mother see eye to eye? What would he think of her budding relationship with Jill?

"You look just beautiful!" he said. "Like always." It was true. His sister's face had matured well, her form was perfect, and she radiated an air of total happiness. "It's very good of you to come to meet me," he added. "I was hoping you would, but I didn't dare to expect it. Typical Syl, always thinking of the others, ever generous."

"I was being selfish, not generous," she laughed. "I just wanted to be the first to see you. I have my car outside. Shall I take you into the city?"

"Perhaps not. I've booked a rental car. I may as well pick it up now."

"That makes sense. Come along. I'll show you where the baggage arrives." They crossed the arrivals hall. "Mum can't wait to see you. I saw her earlier this morning. She's fixed up the guest bedroom for you. Once you have settled in, I hope you will come out to see me at Ardeath."

"With great pleasure. Did Duncan get back safely?" John asked.

"Yes. He went to see Mum yesterday."

They left the terminal building and parted company. John then collected his rental car, an orange Fiat 500 with standard gear shift, and drove into Aberdeen, taking as much care as he could since there were no roads to speak of in Makkovik, and even driving in Goose Bay was very simple as compared to Aberdeen.

On his way in, he passed the street where Duncan had once lived with Ruth before they were married. "Too bad it didn't work out," he said to himself. "Duncan should have waited. There's no point in making a wrong marriage. Later on, everyone suffers."

Turning up into Old Aberdeen, he passed in front of a pub where he and his university pals had often gone after classes. It was still there, looking more upmarket than he recalled.

When he reached his mother's house, the front door was wide open, and his mother was standing there waving vigorously. She must have been out on the doorstep for the last hour! She did look older, but no more so than he had prepared himself to expect. She grabbed him in a tight embrace. "John! It's so wonderful to see you again after all these years. I'm so happy!" She burst into floods of tears.

John was overcome. Suddenly he was happy to be there, there with his mother, there in the land of his childhood, there in the old country. "Mum," he finally managed to say. "I'm so sorry I haven't come before. Will you forgive me?"

"Yes, John," she answered. "I forgive you." They went inside.

The house was orderly and comfortable, and he recognised a number of pieces of furniture which had previously been at Bonnycastle.

"Oh!" said Mary, collapsing into a big armchair. "What a joy it is to see you. My own John! Are you tired? Can I get you a cup of tea or coffee? How long ago is it since you left Saint John's? Have you had something to eat? Here, you sit over there so I can look at you!"

John laughed at her outbursts and took a seat as bidden. "Mum. You look really well. We have a lot of catching up ahead of us, but do you know, what I would really like is to have a shower and a change of clothes. Then a cup of tea would suit me very well."

She stood up. "Follow me. I'll show you to your room. It's upstairs. We have to share a bathroom, I'm afraid, it's not like at Bonnycastle. However, I think the shower is better than the one we had at Bonnycastle."

When John came down from his shower, he felt a new man, and the two of them had a long and animated conversation. She had laid out tea and scones with butter and honey.

"Try this honey," she said. "It comes from Sylvia; she keeps bees. Is it true, as Duncan says, that you live all alone on a river? He showed me some pictures. It looks like a complete wilderness."

John then described for her his wife and children, their house, their visits to Makkovik and Goose Bay, the school where David had attended and where Sheila still had two years to go, and a lot more.

"Are you happy?" his mother asked. "That's the only thing that's really important." It sounded a bit as though she thought that his life was rather unsatisfactory, but that if he was happy, then that was the only thing that mattered.

John smiled. "Of course, I am. As you probably know, Syl met me at the airport. She certainly seems very happy. I would say, in top form. I hope to visit her in a day or so."

"She's a dear. She visits me regularly; I'm very lucky. She has a new friend called Jill, who shares the cottage with her. I'm sure you'll meet her when you go. She's very nice."

"Duncan told me that Syl and he are not on speaking terms. I find that very sad. What happened?"

"As far as I know, it was a silly incident where Duncan made a comment about her not living with a man, preferring women, something of the sort. Sylvia took offence. I think she was quite right to do so. However, that was a while ago, and I'm hoping that your return here will provide an excuse for them to resolve their differences. Will you try to convince Sylvia?"

"Yes, Mum, I'll try."

Mary saw John admiring some roses on a side table. "Sylvia and Jill sent me those. Wasn't that thoughtful of them! And you'll never guess who..."

24

Later on that day, Jessica came to the door of Mary's house, a vase of mixed flowers in her hands. Her heart was bursting; she was so happy. She couldn't wait to see him. The previous night, she had hardly slept. This was going to be one of the most important moments in her life, a turning point, a step forward. She rang the doorbell.

She had put on a white cashmere pullover. It was closely fitting and had a crew neck that perfectly suited her. At her collar was a string of pearls. She hoped that she hadn't overdone the perfume.

What would he look like? How would he find her? She would have liked to brush back a bit of hair that was falling across her forehead but couldn't risk dropping the flowers.

As the door opened in front of her, she took a deep breath. It was John. He looked older, yes, but even more good looking than before: more flesh in the face, broader shoulders, he even seemed taller. "John!" she cried out, offering the flowers to him with an ecstatic smile. "These are for you, a coming home present."

John recognised her immediately but was unable to master his surprise at seeing her so soon after his arrival.

"Jessica!" he exclaimed.

Throughout his journey, John had asked himself if he would or would not try to see Jessica again. He half expected that she would have left Aberdeen, or married, or that in some other way the problem would be solved for him. This had led him to avoid the real question: did he actually wish to see her again? And assuming that he did, was this to be like meeting up again with an old friend? Or would it be more? Would he wish to renew their former relationship, and to what extent?

His hesitations, his indecision, had prevented him from properly anticipating the moment now that it had come. He didn't know how to react, which way to turn, whether to blow hot or cold.

"That's awfully kind of you, Jessica," he said. He found that his voice was failing him and cleared his throat. "Come on in. Please."

She passed through the doorway with her flowers, and they stood together in the front hall looking at each other, appraising each other. Jessica's face positively radiated her joy at seeing him again. "I won't stay long. I have flowers to deliver. Where shall I put them?" She couldn't wait to put the vase down so she could brush that bit of hair out of her face. She hoped he hadn't noticed it.

John took the vase from her. "We can put them here on this table. They're lovely. Thank you so much."

"How do you find me?" she asked him, her hand finally brushing her hair back. "Have I changed much?"

"Jessica, you always were beautiful, and..." Here he was. The moment of truth. He desperately made his choice. Self-control. No hyperbole. "...and you look just as much so today."

Jessica smiled in gratitude. "Thank you, John. And you look wonderful. I'm so happy to see you again!" She spoke with special emphasis and taking a step towards him, tilted her face upwards for a kiss. Her perfume filled the air.

John held her firmly by the shoulders and gave her a

rapid kiss on each cheek.

Jessica was devastated. She was expecting something totally different. She began to consider John's behaviour more closely. Was it possible that he didn't share her feelings, her delight at their coming together again?

She went over to the side table where John had placed the flowers. She expertly rearranged them, rotating the vase slightly to give them maximum effect. She was furiously trying to gather her thoughts together. He watched her closely and was overcome by the grace of her body and of the way she moved.

"I brought some roses to your mother the other day," she said. "They were a gift from your sister and her friend. Tell me, how is your mother? How do you find her?"

"She's in good spirits, thanks. But what a change thirty years can bring! I suppose it does so to us all."

Jessica nodded. "I'm afraid so. I know that your mother will want to see you as much as she can, but I do hope that we can see each other a lot as well. I would really like to hear about your life in Canada. It must be quite exciting, much less boring than life here in Aberdeen." She looked at her watch. "Unfortunately, I have to run. I have a rush order for some flowers in Torphins. Can we see each other again soon?"

John hesitated. "Let's wait and see, Jessica. Please. I have only just arrived. Perhaps later. Right now, I have a whole lot of catching up to do with Mother." Jessica had difficulty concealing her disappointment. "It's nice that you have a flower shop," John added with a smile. "I think that it suits you."

"Well. It puts dinner on the table. Just. My shop is at the top of Union Street, and I live alone in Potterton."

He caught the allusion right away. She was single. Unlike him.

"Why don't you drop by to see the shop?" she continued. "Have you a car? There's an extra parking space beside mine that no one is using just now.”

“Perhaps. Can we speak to each other again at another moment?”

“Yes. My card’s on the flowers. You know where to reach me. Any time.” She paused. “Goodbye for now John.” Her grey eyes met his. She wanted him to take her close, to talk to her, to fill the void in her life.

“Goodbye Jess, and thanks again for the flowers.” John now called her by the name which he had always used before. It gave her a surge of pleasure.

25

He reaches the little ruined cottage first. The day is warm, but the summer sun alternates with dark clouds and there will surely be showers.

"Oh," Jessica says breathlessly as she arrives, "you're here already." They share a long kiss. "My father wouldn't let me alone this morning. I think he was watching me."

"Were you still in the house, or outdoors?" John asks anxiously. He does not want them to be discovered by her father.

"In the house. I think we're alright now. He went up to his office to do some estate work." They kiss again.

The sky darkens. Rain is approaching. They can hear the noise of the raindrops as they hit the leaves in the tops of the trees. The noise is coming closer; it is getting louder and louder. "Come quickly," she says. "Let's get inside." She takes John's hand and leads him into the shelter of the one-room cottage.

John is surprised. "I didn't think it was all fixed up like this inside. Were you here? Did you do this?" The earthen floor is covered with barley straw. A rough wooden table stands to one side. There are two chairs. That's all. But it's clean and

smells fresh.

"Yes. It's nice, isn't it?" Jessica is now seventeen and has reached her full height. Her red hair can reach down to the middle of her back, but today it is loosely tied up and pinned under a tweed cap. Her face is fair and she has a few freckles.

They are both wearing wind jackets. John removes his and throws it onto one of the chairs. "I'm glad to take that off. I was getting warm." Jessica now stands in front of him and loosens her hair; it falls in a golden cascade over her shoulders. She deliberately removes first her jacket and then her pullover. She is wearing nothing underneath, and her breasts seem to pour out of the pullover as she passes it over her head. John is enthralled. He has felt her breasts before under her clothes, but this is the first time he has seen them.

Jessica pulls him to her, they kiss, and she then leads him to a corner where the straw is very fresh and deep, and they lie down side by side. "Have you ever done it before?" she finally asks him.

"No. You?"

She smiles and shakes her head ambiguously, those grey eyes looking steadily into his. As he buries his face in her breasts, she strips off her jeans. John finds that her body has a wonderful smell of fresh grass, even of milk. His mind blurs. He fumbles with his fly. She pulls him closer onto her.

"John," she says, "I love you. More that you can imagine. I'm so happy!" As he starts to enter her, she gives a sharp gasp of pain and grabbing his hand, puts its fleshy bit in her mouth and bites hard. Her feet brace against the straw bedding beneath her and her body pushes up against his.

Together, they share the pain. And together, they share the exultation.

26

Jill parked near the now familiar little gate and walked up to the open garage door. Andrea was at the same table as before. Her face lit up when she saw Jill. "What a nice surprise. Just as I was beginning to get a bit bored with what I was doing."

"My friend likes her painting very much and wanted me to give you this little present." Jill held out a small pot of honey. "She keeps bees. Not as a business," she added. "We only have one hive. It's very good honey, though, much better than what you buy in the shops." She put the honey on the edge of the table.

"That's very kind of her, of both of you. I love honey. Please tell her that I'm very grateful. You said when you came before that you live at Ardeath. Where exactly?"

"In the little cottage near Bonnycastle," Jill answered.

Andrea paused. "I see," she said. "I suspect that you already know, but I once lived on Ardeath as well. Tell me, what is your friend's name?"

"Sylvia. Sylvia Cowan."

"Oh! I always liked Sylvia a lot. She was very sweet. I can't imagine what she would be like today. The last time that I saw her, she must have been eighteen or nineteen." Andrea paused. "Those were not happy times on the estate, and I generally prefer not to think about them."

A breeze had arisen, and Andrea rose to fetch a cardigan and wrap it about her shoulders. Jill also felt slightly cold and shifted her chair to a more sheltered spot. "What are you working on just now?" she asked.

"Some memories of Ireland. I think that I told you that I was brought up in Limerick. It's a lovely old city, and I was thinking about how I might work some of my memories from back then into a new painting that I have started. I still have two sisters living in Ireland, Meabh and Siobhan. They are both married and have children, so I have a lot of family there. Still, my own son and daughter live here, and here I stay."

Jill's face lit up. "Those are beautiful names, Meabh and Siobhan. Very different from Andrea."

Andrea laughed. "I was born first, but my father died when I was young and my mother remarried. Her second husband was a *muinteoir*, a teacher of Irish. He chose the names. Siobhan means God is gracious; Meabh was an ancient warrior queen. Where are you from originally?"

"Glasgow, but I have no family there now. My parents separated when I was eight years old. I continued living with my mother and we saw very little of my father after that. Then, when I was twenty-two, my mother died of breast cancer. It was a great shock, a great loss for me."

"What made you come up here?"

"This past summer, I met Sylvia and we immediately clicked. She is my family now."

"Yes, it's hard to be alone," Andrea said thoughtfully.

"You know, I was thinking that we should exchange phone numbers. I really enjoy talking to you, and perhaps you enjoy my visits as well. Would you like that?"

"That is a wonderful idea. Of course, I would. Let's do it."

Jill changed subjects. "I expect that you recall Sylvia's brother John. He just arrived two days ago from Canada, where he has lived for the last thirty years. He is staying with his mother in Old Aberdeen.”

“John Cowan! His mother must be very pleased. Of course, I remember John. He used to see a lot of my daughter Jessica. I liked him a lot. Not my husband, however. He would become very angry when Jessica and John saw each other. Is John over for long?”

“Three weeks, I believe.”

“What sort of life has he been leading in Canada? I always admired John for going to university. I wish my son Keith had done so as well.” Andrea frowned at the thought. “Is John using his university qualification in some way? I believe it was in botany.”

“I can’t really tell you. All that I know is that he lives up on the Labrador coast. I have not yet met him and am really looking forward to doing so. Sylvia is very excited; I think that they were very close.”

“Personally, I never had anything against the Cowans. I can’t say that we were particularly friendly with each other. After all, they were our tenants, and here in Scotland there can be barriers between the laird and his tenants, much more so I would say than you would find in Ireland. One of the advantages now of my living in the city is that there aren’t any such considerations.”

“I think that things really started to go badly for the Cowans when Sylvia’s father took to drink.”

“It apparently killed him. After that, I can remember my husband and our son discussing at dinner how best to terminate the tenancy at Bonnycastle. I’m not sure they were very fair in the manner in which it was accomplished. Keith was hoping to get a higher rent, I know, and Gerald was happy to see the back end of John, which of course is not quite the way it worked out.”

“No. I gather that John and your daughter were deeply in love with each other and that it went on for quite some time.”

"You're absolutely right. You seem to know a lot about these matters. No doubt then you have heard about the time when John punched my husband on the nose." Andrea threw up her hands. "It was epic! I was in the kitchen, and Jessica came to get me. She was as white as a sheet. 'Come quickly, Mother,' she said. 'Dad and John are having a fight.'"

Jill got the impression that Andrea was actually enjoying telling the story, as if she had been on John's side.

"We went together into the dining room and Gerald was on the floor bleeding from the nose. Jessica told John to leave at once, not I think because she was angry with him, but simply in order to stop the fight there and then. He left. Jessica fetched some ice to put on my husband's nose and the three of us went to the local infirmary to have it attended to. What a donnybrook!"

"I don't suppose John ever returned to the big house after that."

"Not to the house, but he and Jessica were still seeing each other, mostly, I think, in Aberdeen. However, I know for sure of one instance when they met on the estate." Andrea paused. "Am I boring you? If so, please tell me."

Jill encouraged her. "No. Please go ahead."

Andrea's face looked sad. "About a year later, my husband died. It was on October 10, 1992. That's when I last saw John out on the estate." Andrea again hesitated.

"I wish you would tell me about what happened on that day," Jill said, her eyes seeking Andrea's. "I know it must be very difficult for you. However, I would really like to know."

"If you wish," Andrea said. "On that day, my husband announced at lunch that he intended to do a bit of rough shooting in the afternoon. There was nothing unusual about this, as he often went out after lunch with his gun and his spaniel Topper. My son Keith was with us but declined to join him. Keith had been working that morning in the estate office, clearing up some old files. Jessica had disappeared shortly after breakfast.”

“Perhaps to meet John.”

“In fact, yes. As I learned later, she had driven down to Ellon to pick him up at the bus stop and they had come back for a walk together on the estate. After lunch, Gerald went out for his walk, Keith went off somewhere else and I cleaned up.”

“Do you know where Keith went?”

“Upstairs, at first. Then I lost track of him for a while. He may have stayed all that time in the house, or he may have gone outside for a while and then returned. I just can’t say for sure.”

“What did you do after cleaning up?”

“I went upstairs to one of the bedrooms on the top floor. It was a warm sunny day, and I wanted to open the window as the room wanted a bit of airing. I leaned out of the window to admire the view and caught sight of Jessica over by the kennels. She and John were there together, getting into her car. Not a minute later I heard a single shot, the shot that must have killed my husband.”

“Did it come from over by the kennels?”

“No. It came from the other side of the house, from over near that long brick wall that encloses the grounds around the house. Where we found Gerald, eventually. I thought nothing of the shot at first, of course, and continued with my housework. It was only later on that afternoon that Keith came to see me and asked me where his father was.”

“Were you still upstairs?”

“No, by then I was down in the library by the fire having a cup of tea. Jessica came in looking as fresh as a daisy, and had one as well. Then Keith arrived and said that he would go outside to see if his father had shot anything.”

“How long after that was it before you learned of the accident?”

“Not long. Keith returned shortly afterwards and said that his father was nowhere to be seen. I had finished my tea and felt like a bit of fresh air, so I said, 'let's go out together and find him'. We went over to that side of the house where I had heard the shot, and Keith went a bit ahead of me. Suddenly, he stopped, and I could see his hand fly up to his mouth. He turned towards me and shouted, 'Mummy, Mummy! There's been a horrible accident! Call an ambulance! Call the police!' He had just come across his father's body. Gerald was lying there in a pool of blood." Andrea shook her head as if in disbelief. "It was terrible to see."

Jill softly asked, "and where was Topper?"

Andrea looked slightly startled. "Topper? He had stayed with Gerald the whole while. He only came back to the house when we went to call the police."

27

John called and told Sylvia that he was on his way. He brought with him a good bottle of wine that he had bought duty free at the airport

It was wonderful to drive out of the city and recognise the old familiar spots along the way, even with their numerous changes. The roads were certainly much better. He found the trees stunning: there was nothing to rival them for height and luxuriance in Labrador.

When he reached the village, he recognised the square, the pond and he even detected a faint smell of peat smoke in the air. He loved that smell. He turned up the little road leading to the estate, passed in front of the main gate on the drive leading up to the big house, and finally came to a small cottage. "This must be Sylvia's," he thought, and turned in.

There she was on the doorstep waiting for him, a broad smile on her face.

"John! Hello again!"

"Ah Syl, what a joy!" They embraced and then stood there examining each other. She was the first to break the spell.

"What an awful colour," she said, pointing at his car. "Orange! Weren't they able to give you something else?"

He grinned. "It works, Syl, it works. After all, it got me here. I rather like the colour, now that I've become used to it. What is rather more difficult to get used to is the size. In Labrador, we generally drive a pickup truck."

"Wait a moment, and I'll call Jill. Are you going to put on a wind jacket? It may get cold today." She disappeared into the house. John returned to the car to put on some boots and an extra layer, and she and Jill eventually emerged, ready for their walk. John and Jill were introduced, and instinctively liked each other.

"Syl," John said to his sister, "you're looking terrific. I should add that you also look very happy. There is a wonderful sparkle in your eyes."

"Thank you, John," she replied. "I have plenty of reason to be happy, just seeing you again. We were pretty close when you left. You were the classic older brother."

He grinned. "And you, the classic baby sister!"

Sylvia laughed. "I was in awe of you. You could do no wrong." She paused. "I missed you a lot afterwards. Your departure was rather brutal, you know."

"Yes, it was, and I'm sorry. To be fair, however, I had been thinking seriously about emigrating for some time. It's just that I never discussed it with anybody. Do you find me changed?"

"It would be too early to tell. Probably more than me, living in Labrador, being married, having children. Yes, you must certainly have changed in some ways, but for me, you still look like the same old John." She paused. "Almost, in any event."

They all laughed and set out along the road, chatting happily.

The night before, Jill had told Sylvia about her conversation with Andrea, in particular regarding Gerald's death. Jill was now bursting to let John know. After all, it made it very clear that John was in no way responsible for

Gerald's death. It was delicate, however. She didn't want John to think that she had ever doubted in his innocence, and perhaps he was so confident of that fact that he wouldn't even be interested in hearing Andrea's story. So yes, it was delicate.

"John. Jill has recently struck up an acquaintance with Andrea Symons. Jill, you should tell John what you told me last night about Gerald Symons' death."

"All right," Jill said, drawing closer to the others so that they could hear. "I went to call on Andrea. We have sort of become friends, and she told me a bit about her husband's death."

"What did she say?" asked John. Even though he hadn't thought much about the matter for a very long time, he could recall every detail of that dramatic day.

"She told me that on the afternoon that Gerald died, she was upstairs at the front of the house and opened a window. Looking out, she saw you getting into a car." She paused, looking at John expectantly.

"Yes. Into Jessica's car. That must have been when she took me back to Ellon to catch the bus." He remembered that drive with her all too well. Jessica had sharply criticised her father and complained bitterly about the atmosphere at home.

Jill continued. "Where were you both at the time? Where was the car parked?"

"At the kennels."

"Correct. A short moment after, Andrea heard the shot that killed Gerald. It came from the other side of the house, where they eventually found Gerald."

"A long way away from me."

"Correct again."

John took a deep breath and thought for a while about the implications of what Jill had said. "Thank you, Jill. It's good to know that. Even if the police concluded that Gerald died in an accident, I'm sure that some people may have thought that he was murdered."

John didn't realise it, but Jill was also reassured by their conversation. His version of the facts agreed with that of Andrea. Both were therefor reliable sources.

They walked on until Sylvia broke the silence. "Do you think that Duncan enjoyed his trip?" she asked.

John laughed and told them about Duncan's mishap coming down the river. Sylvia gasped. "He could easily have drowned!"

"He handled himself pretty well. Actually, apart from his accident, I think that he enjoyed Labrador a lot." John's face became more serious. "I don't know what to make of Duncan, though; he doesn't seem to me to be all that happy. I think he needs to find himself a new life."

"You're right there," said Sylvia. "Perhaps he will. Apparently, he has been in contact with Mum's brother Gordon, and may buy an interest in his trawler."

She stopped to point up the hill. "Look John! There's Bonnycastle."

"Yes, I can see it. Everything looks very much the same. It's as though nothing has changed."

With a broad grin, Sylvia then pointed across a field to a small ruin. "And that's where you used to meet Jessica."

"How do you know?" John asked sharply.

"Of course, I know. We all knew. I used to spy on you! I must have been good at it if you never noticed."

"You're lucky Jessica never noticed. She would have made you regret it!"

"I don't remember her that way. You make her sound like a virago!"

"I was on the phone with her a day or two ago," said Jill, "and she sounded very nice. She seemed particularly interested in your news, John."

John blushed. How come Jill had been on the phone with Jessica? What was going on behind his back?

"Mum says that she brought you some flowers," Sylvia

teased. "That's what I would call special attention. Perhaps she remembered about your interest in botany."

"Syl," John was red in the face. "It isn't funny. I have come back to see Mum, to see you. Not, emphatically not to see Jessica."

That put a temporary end to the subject. They rounded the corner by the wall and started to head towards the gates on the main drive leading up to the big house.

Sylvia attempted to soothe John's wounded feelings. "Do you hunt animals back in Labrador?"

"As little as possible," was the curt reply.

Jill tried in turn. "Is there a school for your children?"

"Yes, of course," John said.

"I would really like to go out there some time," Jill said. "It must be very beautiful."

John was mollified. "You should come, Jill. I think Labrador would be particularly suited to you."

"In what way?" she asked.

"You look at home in the outdoors. You seem very physical, very athletic."

Sylvia exploded in laughter. "She certainly is!" Jill gave her an enquiring look. More silence followed.

John was thinking again about what Jill had said about Gerald's death. "Tell me, Jill, we still don't know what happened, though, do we, when Gerald died. Was it an accident, as the police claimed? Can it be that he was murdered? Did he commit suicide? Have you a theory?"

They walked on for a while. Jill finally broke the silence. "I don't think it was murder," she said, "in any event, not by Keith."

Sylvia looked up. "Why not?" she asked. Jill had said nothing to her before about this.

John was also interested. He had never liked Keith and had occasionally fantasised that Keith might have eliminated his father in order to accede to the estate.

"Well, Andrea told me that when she heard the shot, she thought nothing of it. After all, her husband was out with his gun precisely in the hope of shooting the odd pheasant. She finished what she was doing upstairs and then went down to the library to have a cup of tea. Eventually, Jessica joined her. It was only a while afterwards that Keith appeared and asked where his father was. Andrea didn't know, so Keith went to the back door to have a look. He then returned to say that his father was nowhere to be seen. Andrea felt like a walk, so she and Keith set out to find Gerald."

"Who was dead by this time," added Sylvia.

"Yes. He would have died an hour or two previously. The time it took for Jessica to take John to Ellon and then return."

"But was Andrea aware of Keith's whereabouts at the time Gerald died?" John asked.

"No. It is clear that Keith would have had the opportunity to go out, shoot his father and return to the house."

They both looked at Jill. Sylvia was the first to ask. "So what makes you say that Keith didn't murder his father?"

Jill spoke with an enigmatic smile on her face. "I had the idea thinking about Jock's dog and about how she behaved the other day. She's a black Lab. These working dogs are very obedient, very faithful; it really struck me at the time."

She had their attention. What was she getting at? They both looked at her expectantly.

"When Andrea and Keith found Gerald's dead body, Gerald's dog Topper was there beside him. It seems highly likely that he hadn't moved since the time of Gerald's death about two hours previously. Andrea told me that Topper did follow them back to the house, however, when they returned in order to call the police."

Sylvia and John waited expectantly.

"In my opinion," Jill continued, "if Keith had killed his father, if he had gone out, fired the shot, put the gun at the side of his father's body and returned to the house afterwards,

Topper would have gone back to the house with him."

"You may have something there, Jill," said Sylvia. "That dog used to go out with Keith as well. I can remember seeing them together."

"Yes," Jill continued. "He would have followed Keith back to the house and Andrea would have found him at the mudroom door when she went out with Keith. But no, Gerald and Topper were alone together when Gerald died, and Topper stayed there alone beside his master until Andrea and Keith appeared. Only when they went back to the house to call the police did he go back with them."

The three had stopped walking and stood there in the middle of the road. John and Sylvia remained motionless, totally absorbed by Jill's explanation. When she concluded, they both took deep breaths.

"I think you're right, Jill" said John. He was beginning to see that there was another side to Jill, that she had a knack for analysis, for getting to the bottom of things. "Yes, Jill," he nodded, "you must be right."

"So, it was probably an accident or suicide," said Sylvia. "Which was it, Jill?"

"I'm not sure yet, but I'm getting there."

28

"John!" Jessica exclaimed. She was surprised to see him so soon after their previous conversation. Her face lit up in a broad smile as she spread her arms in a gesture of welcome.

John stood there in the street, looking slightly awkward. He held out the vase which his mother had suggested he return. "Mum wanted me to return this vase to you, Jess. She is delighted to have all those flowers! She says that her house has never looked so fine."

"Come on in," she said. "It's marvellous to see you again."

Returning into the shop with the vase, she held the door open for him. When they were inside, she set the vase on the counter. "We always seem to be carrying flowers to each other, John, flowers or vases." She laughed happily. Perhaps her impression from the first time they had seen each other was wrong. Or perhaps John had changed his mind. Either way, here he was and her hopes were rising rapidly.

"Tell me, is it good to be back in Scotland? Are you pleased to see me again? Does it bring back old memories?" She closed the door behind them.

John examined the shop with approval. "Yes, I'm happy to be back. It really is good to see Mum again, and Sylvia and

Duncan. And of course, I'm happy to see you too, Jess."

For her, it was so simple, he reflected. She could take him, body and soul. Like in the old days. She had no conflicting obligations. His position was entirely different. He owed a loyalty to Melba, to their children and to the home they had built back in Labrador. He realised with a start that somehow, his life and family in Canada now seemed distant, as if all of that had happened in another life.

Somehow, these various thoughts were reflected in his eyes and on his face. In turn, he looked bewildered, he looked resolute, he looked sad. Jessica saw all of this. She led him to a table and two chairs by the window, and they sat down opposite each other. She examined him in the sunlight which filtered in from outside. "I'm trying to remember how you used to look," she said. "Your hair was always a mess. You wore round spectacles that made you look like an owl."

They both laughed, but both were feeling nervous. The conversation that they were initiating was one for which neither had a script. "And now?" John asked. "Now, how do I look?"

"Now you look very handsome, very respectable, a bit weather worn." She looked at him closely. "I like you even more now."

"Perhaps your tastes have changed," John said. "After all, we're both older now."

Jessica did not wish to be reminded that she had aged. She still felt young and certainly did look younger than most of her contemporaries. "I still have all my hair," she teased him; "on the other hand..." she reached up to stroke his forehead where the hairline had started to recede.

Her face lit up. "Do you remember the walks we used to take in Seaton Park when you were at university? And that pub just outside the Powis Gates? And the trip we made to Paris after you graduated? We were so happy then!" Her expression changed. "It has never been the same for me since you left."

"I'm truly sorry if that's so, Jess. I really am." John reached out across the table and touched her hand softly. "I also want you to know that I have always felt ashamed at the way we parted. I feel that I owe you an apology. A big apology." He looked uncomfortable.

"You mean your letter?" she asked.

"Yes. That letter. I shouldn't have written it at all. I should have sat down with you and explained everything." His voice faltered and he stared at his hands. "It is the thing in my life of which I am the most ashamed, which I most regret."

"Yes, it was cowardly of you after all that we had shared. We went out five years together. I never gave myself to anyone else, not even in Italy." Jessica looked hard at him. "Then you left me without a word."

"I'm sorry." He looked up. His mind went back to the days following Gerald's death. The police had been in to see him in Aberdeen at least twice. They had quizzed him about his presence at Ardeath that fatal afternoon. Where had he been? Had he seen anything? What was his relationship with Jessica? Why had he had that fight with Gerald? Did he take drugs? It had gone on and on, almost driving him crazy, as if he was a criminal, as if he was in some way responsible for Gerald's death. He had decided that enough was enough, that he wanted nothing further to do with the Symons family, with Ardeath, with Scotland. He didn't want to say all this to her, no not now. "I'm really sorry Jess," was all that he could manage.

"If you and I had only met to discuss it, the outcome might have been different," she said.

"I don't think so." He shifted on his chair.

She looked at him closely. "If you had chosen to explain yourself to me, what would you have said?"

John took a deep breath. This wasn't going to be easy. "Jess. I suppose that I would have said several things, and in no particular order. I would have said that I wanted to start a new life. That I wasn't satisfied with myself. I found myself weak, a follower. Not one who chose his own direction, but one who let himself be carried along by circumstance."

"Is that all?" Jessica asked.

"No. I would have said that I didn't want to be a farmer. I didn't even want to be an academic. I wanted something challenging, but also something outdoors that would toughen me up."

"Hence, Canada," she said.

"Yes. Hence, Canada. I never told you, but I had been thinking about Canada for some time."

Jessica became angry. "You should have told me. I would have been the first to want to leave Scotland. I absolutely hated staying at home. My father was constantly nagging at me and my mother was switched off, like she was in another world. They barely ever spoke to each other anymore. The atmosphere was poisonous. I would have gone to Canada with you in a flash."

John hesitated. "Jess. I also wanted to leave alone. Without you. You were ready to make a permanent choice. I wasn't. You were far more mature than I was. I wanted to remain single, I wasn't ready to get married."

Jessica was aware of the fact that John had since married; she had learned that through the grapevine some time ago. "When was it that you did get married?"

John thought. "About ten years later."

"Why didn't you stay in touch with me? Why didn't you come back to see me?"

"I don't know, Jess. I'm sorry. I just don't know."

She was puzzled. Which way was their conversation heading? Was John about to tell her that his marriage was finished and that he wanted to return to her or was he about to explain to her why he did not want them to come back together. "What's your wife like?"

"Melba? She's very steady, reliable, understanding. She has a good head on her shoulders. She is an excellent wife and mother."

Jessica's face flushed red as her hopes sank. "I see," she murmured.

"But tell me, Jess," John said. "What about you? What did you do after I left?"

"I'll tell you," she said angrily, looking up at him through sparkling eyes. "When you left, I was disoriented. I lost all interest in living, in life itself. I stumbled through Dad's funeral. Then Keith more or less kicked Mum and me out of the house. That's what I did after you left."

"And later, did things get better? Have you had a happy life?" he asked hopefully.

Jessica became even more emotional. "I got various jobs. I had various men in my life. Nothing ever seemed to work out. It's all too tedious to tell you, John. Please spare me the pain."

Tears suddenly came to her eyes and then she broke down completely. "I'm sorry, John. I can't help it," she sobbed. "I feel so miserable. I'm so unhappy. Please forgive me. Let me cry for a minute or two, then I'll be alright."

John waited while she held a tissue to her eyes and attempted to calm herself. He felt helpless.

"How long have you had the flower shop?" he finally asked her.

"Five or six years now. I bought my little house in Potterton at about the same time." Jessica swallowed hard. She reached for another tissue and blew her nose. "I would love to show it to you," she said through her tears.

John suddenly felt very sad for Jessica, and very tired. Life could be so cruel. Good luck was so unevenly distributed.

"What about your mother? How long did you live with her?"

Her voice rose in anger. "Not long. If you must know, I moved in with a man I met through my job. I had work as a legal secretary, and he was a solicitor in the firm. That lasted a few years. Then I rented for a while and lived alone."

"And then you bought the house in Potterton?"

"No. There was a period when I lived out in the country in a friend's house. He was married, but we were very close, and so he let me have a small house near his own." Jessica paused, white as a sheet. "You see, mine is a desolate tale."

She gazed out the window, her mind in turmoil, but gradually recovering her composure. "John, over all these years, I have never stopped loving you." Their eyes met, hers still bleary, and his, uneasy, even alarmed. "In a way, that has been my problem. But in a way, it has also sustained me."

She felt an overpowering need to be with him, to let her emotions run their course. If it couldn't be for ever, perhaps at least it could be for a few days...

Pointing at the ring on John's left hand, she gave him a hesitant smile. "You wouldn't want to take it off, just for a few days, would you?"

John blinked. "What?"

"Your wedding ring, John. Just put it somewhere safe, in a drawer. I have a proposition to make to you." Jessica was regaining confidence. She was feeling a little more like her old self.

John was wary. "I don't think I like what you are suggesting, Jessica."

"Listen to me, John," she said. "I have a plan. Let's go away together for a night or two where no one can see us." John started to say something. "No. Hear me out," she ordered. "I promise you; I'll not attempt to destroy your marriage. At the end, we'll simply shake hands and say goodbye."

"Jessica," he started to say, but again, she silenced him.

"For a day or two, we'll be like we used to be. We'll talk endlessly to each other, explain our emotions, our lives. Go for walks together. Laugh and cry. We'll kiss all we want. We'll make love whenever we feel like it. We'll be hedonists for the moment, eat good food, drink good wine. At the end, it will have been nothing but a dream, and we'll return to life as usual, as though nothing had happened." Jessica was transported. She found the idea irresistible.

"No, Jess," was all that John could say.

"John," she said. "Be honest." She reached a hand across the table and touched his hand lightly. "You can be honest, can't you? Then tell me. Is my idea tempting? Are you tempted? Would you like us to spend a short while together on those terms?"

"Jessica," John finally managed to say. "Of course, your idea is tempting. You are a wonderful person. I once was deeply in love with you. This is all so. But I think that I have the both the right and the obligation to refuse the temptation. And it would be more in character for me to refuse it. After all, we are very different, you and I. You are warm-blooded and passionate. I am more measured, perhaps even cold."

"You weren't cold when we were lovers," came the reply. "You too were impetuous and passionate. What makes you different now?"

John reflected that perhaps "marriage" was the answer. For a moment, he was tempted to say so, and risk Jessica's scorn. "We were younger then," was finally his answer. It was not much better, but it would have to do.

The expression on Jessica's face began to change. She withdrew her hand from John's and looked at him mockingly. "Poor you, John. You've grown old."

She tried to hide her real feelings. She felt discouraged, hurt, even desperate. It was like when he had left her the first time. However, he hadn't left Scotland yet. Perhaps her words would sink in. Perhaps his defences would soften.

29

Duncan grabbed a warm wind jacket and headed for his car. He was in high spirits. "Here we go, Duncan me boy!" he said to himself out loud. "Off to the Broch. Soon you'll be a fisherman!"

He was on his way north to meet up with his uncle Gordon. They were to take the *Sunset Sea* down the coast from Fraserburgh to Peterhead, where she was to have her engines checked.

Fraserburgh was about an hour's drive away, and when he reached the harbour, he could see a forest of trawlers tied up to the jetties and sometimes to each other. Perhaps the weather was going to turn and the fishing fleet was taking shelter. He found parking, put his jacket on, and went to look for the *Sunset Sea*.

The boats all looked somewhat similar to him, so he had to ask. He finally located her and went alongside. His two cousins, Bill and Jim, were tying something down on the deck and, seeing him, gave him a warm welcome.

"Come on board, Duncan. Gordon's below."

He jumped over the rail on to the deck. Everything was in perfect order. Going down the narrow stairs into the galley, he found his uncle fixing up some sandwiches. "Welcome, Duncan. You're a bit early, which is good because it means we can leave right away." He finished with the sandwiches and went up to the pilothouse. "Get ready to cast off, boys. We're leaving."

The trip down to Peterhead was a short one, and as the tide was rising, they didn't have to go too far out to sea to round Rattray Head. Bill took the wheel, and Gordon showed Duncan the boat.

"She has a steel hull and was built in Macduff in 1987. Twenty-three metres long. The engine is a Cummins and was recently overhauled. She has a three drum winch and a double net drum. Down below there's an ice machine for the fish. The electronics are modern, and we have all the necessary certificates. She's a good boat, really."

As they talked, Gordon expressed enthusiasm about Duncan's buying his share. Bill and Jim were fishermen first and foremost. Duncan, with his business experience, would make a good partner for them, as operating a trawler was more than just that; it was also running a fair-sized business. You needed to finance operations, schedule maintenance, comply with all sorts of regulations, take on crew, and so forth. Finding experienced crew was one of the big challenges; it was dangerous to go to sea with unreliable crew members.

"I'll only make one condition," said Gordon to Duncan. "I still want to come out on her from time to time, just to help, without getting in the way."

They were well underway now, and Duncan was feeling on top of the world. This was to be his new life. There was a cold wind blowing, and the swell became so strong he had to grasp the rail. Gordon seemed to think it was just another sunny afternoon. They came abreast of the Rattray Light, set amongst dunes of swaying bent grass, with broad fields and little bits of wood lying beyond. Further to the south, the entrance to Peterhead harbour came into sight.

SUNSET SEA

A few minutes later, they headed in. A spot awaited them over by the engineering facility, and they went alongside and tied up. After some discussions with the mechanic, they jumped into a Volkswagen minibus and were driven back to Fraserburgh. Duncan thanked Gordon, said he would call him in a day or so in order to make a formal offer, and returned to his car.

He glanced at his cell phone. There was a message from Sylvia. Of all people! What could she want? They hadn't spoken for a long while. With real curiosity and a certain amount of apprehension, he returned her call.

"Duncan," she answered. "It's been a long time."

"Sylvia. I am really happy you called. Yes, it has been a long time. Far too long."

"Mum says that you're up at the Broch."

"Yes I am. Just about to head home. I had a nice boat ride down to Peterhead with Gordon and the boys."

"Have you time to drop by here on your way back to Aberdeen? It would be good for us to have a little chat, don't you think?"

"Gladly. I'm leaving just now. I can be there in about forty minutes. You are at your home right now?"

"Yes I am. See you soon."

As he drove south, Duncan thought back to the comment that he had made to Sylvia three years ago and that had so soured their relationship. It had been an incredibly stupid thing to say. Gratuitous and simply wrong.

It was not as though he and Sylvia had ever been that close. She and John had always stuck together, leaving Duncan to one side. However, he had never wished to insult her, and her private life was simply none of his business. Anyway, who was he to judge?

He arrived at the cottage and knocked at the door. Sylvia appeared and stood there in the doorway.

"Well, Duncan," she said guardedly. "I suppose we may as

well stay out of doors. Will you be warm enough?" She herself was wearing a heavy sweater.

"Hang on. I'll put my coat on." He fetched his wind jacket out of the car. "It was cold out there on the boat. I'm very happy you called, Syl."

"Both Mother and John have been after me, and I guess we should make our peace." She looked somewhat unconvinced.

"I agree," said Duncan. "It's my fault entirely, and I apologise. What I said to you at the time was stupid and I now regret it. It was completely wrong to say what I said."

"You know. You really don't know anything about my private life," she said, putting the screws on him a bit. "You had no basis on which to judge me."

"You're right, Syl."

"Even if you did, it would have been morally wrong of you to say what you said."

"Yes. Of course."

There was a short silence. Sylvia smiled mischievously. "It just so happens that I have a friend living with me just now. She and I have become very close. In fact, we love each other. We also sleep together. Do you find that wicked?" Sylvia was surprised by her boldness. She had never been assertive like this before.

"Sylvia. I promise you I now understand. It's not my business. Except, of course," he added, "that my one wish for you is that you should be happy. Syl, you are opening my eyes. Thanks for that. Please, let's turn the page."

"OK. I agree." Sylvia was prepared to let the matter drop. She felt that she had now made her point.

"Thank you, Syl, and again, my apologies." Duncan felt a heavy load had lifted from his shoulders.

Sylvia brought the conversation back to the present. "How were Gordon and the boys? Do you really think that you will buy a share of their boat?"

"It looks highly likely, Syl. We are talking about a one-third interest for roughly three hundred thousand pounds. I can raise that easily enough by selling my house. You are our fishing expert in the family. Would you buy into a fishing boat at this time?"

"That's a difficult question. The fish stocks are there, and with Brexit, Scotland should be increasing its fishing rights. But fish need a market, just like any other produce, and ideally, a market that is readily accessible, like the EU. This is where our negotiations with Europe are so critical. Until we have reached a new deal, it's unclear what the future of the Scottish fishing industry will be."

"When do you think that we'll know? You seem to have been following the negotiations."

Sylvia laughed. "I sure have been. That's about all I've been working on for the last six months. We'll know on December thirty-first, and perhaps not even then."

"So would you do the deal with Gordon?" Duncan asked.

"Yes," she said simply. "I would."

"John thinks so as well. Isn't it wonderful that he decided to come back?"

"Yes, it is. Congratulations for pulling it off. That must have been a fascinating trip that you made."

"It was, actually. I'll tell you about it some time. What is John's news? Have you seen him? I've hardly spoken to him since his return. Is he happy to be back? He and Mum must be spending a lot of time together, reminiscing like mad."

Sylvia smiled. "No doubt. He was out here the other day and we had a good long walk. He seems to be enjoying his trip. He even has caught up with Jessica. Or vice versa."

Duncan laughed. "Probably both."

30

Jill turned off the A948 into New Deer. It was a well-ordered little town: rows and rows of substantial stone cottages, one or two churches, a few shops. Jill hoped to find out more about those taxi rides that Margaret Downie used to take thirty years ago. At the Post Office, she had found some old directories, and the name of the taxi service: Melrose Taxis. She had an address for a Mr Melrose and stopped in front of his house near the village square.

He answered the door at once. He was plump and vivacious, well on in years, but not the worse for it. His face was round and his eyes bulged like those of a goldfish. "Mr Melrose?"

"Yes. That's me. Can I help you?"

"Mr Melrose..." Jill started. He interrupted her. "Please. Please call me Andy."

Jill started again. "Thanks Andy. My name's Jill. Jill Brown. I live just outside Ellon and am looking into some events that occurred down there some thirty years ago. Do you mind if I ask you a question or two?"

"Not at all. Glad to be of service. Come on in." Andy rolled his 'r's on the tip of his tongue and had a slight lisp. If he was curious about why Jill wanted to ask him questions, he didn't show it. In fact, hers was a pleasant and unexpected interruption to his day. He wasn't going to spoil that. They sat down in his living room.

"I believe that you had a taxi service here in New Deer in the early 1990s."

"That's right. I retired about ten years ago." Andy leaned forward in his chair. "Can I offer you a cup of tea?"

Jill smiled. "No thanks. That's very kind, but I don't want to take up too much of your morning. But tell me, were you the only driver or did someone else drive for you as well?"

Andy leaned back, and reflected. "It was mostly me. Sometimes I had help though."

"Who else drove for you?" Jill thought that this was beginning to look promising.

"One or two of the lads. But mostly, it was Nora. Nora Settle. She was a neighbour of mine at the time."

Jill's thoughts raced ahead. A woman driving the taxi! This would fit nicely with what Jock had told her. "You say 'At the time'. Is she still alive?"

"No," Andy replied. "Unfortunately, she died two or three years ago."

At first, Jill felt discouraged, but then she thought that perhaps if Nora Settle was dead, Andy might feel more free to say something of interest. She continued. "So, Nora drove as well. Did she have her own clients, or did she simply replace you when you asked her?"

"Both," was the reply. "She did both." Andy thought for a while and corrected himself. "Now I think of it, she mostly had her own clients."

"Can you remember who her clients were?"

He hesitated, and appeared somewhat uncomfortable. "She dealt a lot with a woman who lived down towards Aberdeen. Not far from Ellon, in fact."

"Called Margaret Downie?"

He gave Jill a look of surprise. "Yes. That was her name, I think."

"That's odd, though. Why would someone living down near Ellon use the services of a taxi driver based in New Deer?" Jill waited expectantly as Andy pondered his reply.

"She didn't always drive Margaret Downie. She sometimes had other passengers." He paused.

Jill gave it some thought. "Were his passengers usually women?" she finally asked. "Young women?"

"Yes, in fact." Andy could see where Jill was heading. "I never did those trips. Nora booked them, and she kept the fares. Really, she was just using my car."

"I understand," said Jill. "Do you mind if I ask just one more question? Were Nora's trips at regular hours, during daytime I mean?"

"No," Andy replied, thankful that the questions were coming to an end. "They were at all hours of the day. Sometimes she would leave at five in the afternoon and only return at six the next morning."

Jill thanked Andy and rose from her chair. She was very satisfied with what she had learned. Clearly, Margaret had been running some kind of a prostitution ring out here in the Aberdeenshire countryside. It remained for Jill to find out more about Margaret's connection with Gerald Symons. Why, as Jock had told her, had they quarrelled shortly before Gerald died? Then, and only then, would she be able to piece together a full account of his death.

"Good going, Jill," she said to herself as she turned onto the A948 going south. "Wait until you tell Syl about this!"

31

At five o'clock, John placed his call to Canada. He hoped Melba wouldn't notice, but his nerves were fraught. He was supposed to be back in Scotland visiting his mother and his sister. However, the uncomfortable truth was that he had also seen Jessica on two occasions, and that she was never far from his thoughts.

This unnerved him, put him on edge. He liked harmony in his life, no unknowns, no extraneous bits. He prided himself on the fact that he always had things under control. Now Jessica was upsetting everything.

He heard the receiver being picked up at the other end. "Hello, is that you Melba?"

"Jack! Your voice is so clear. It's as though you were in the next room! Where are you, at your mother's?"

"Yes, I'm at her house."

"And how is she?"

"She seems completely over the virus. She hasn't had any symptoms since I arrived, come to think of it."

"You did well to go. You're well? And Duncan and your sister?"

"Yes, thanks. We're all well. Duncan thinks he may invest

in a fishing boat with some cousins. Sylvia and I went for a long walk the other day and she seems very happy. What is your news?"

While Melba told him about David down in Goose Bay starting a course in mechanics, about Sheila starting school and taking private French lessons after classes, and about how the weather was turning towards winter, John couldn't help comparing her familiar, almost flat Labrador accent to the warm Scottish tones of Jessica's voice. He nervously shifted the receiver from one hand to the other. He felt that he was becoming impatient. "Well, we had better stop now," he finally said to Melba, "or my mother's phone bill will get too high."

"When will you be back?" she asked. She was detecting something funny in his voice, something unusual.

"I should be home in about two weeks."

"Be careful, Jack. be careful."

"Why be careful?"

"I had a dream. A bad dream. Just you be careful, I won't say any more."

"What did you dream about?"

"I don't know. I can't even remember. Just that it was a bad dream."

"Don't worry. I'm always careful. You take care of yourself and give my love to David and Sheila."

"Shall do. Love you, Jack."

"Love you, Melba." He rang off.

32

Jessica walks up the stairs to the room where John boards in Aberdeen. She is tense, a bundle of nerves. She hasn't seen John for almost a year. He is now in his second year at university, studying botany. He is waiting for her at the top of the stairs.

"Oh, it's good to see you again, Jess," he cries. "You found me!" They come together passionately, and all the emotions repressed over the last twelve months are unleashed.

"You gave me good directions." She is relieved to find that he is so happy to see her again. "You look wonderful, John. You are just as I remembered you."

"Have you picked up a bit of Italian?" he asks.

"*Un pochino*," she replies. "I can also count in Italian, say here is your bill Madam, and put off unwanted advances by saying that I have a *fidanzato*, which means that I already have a boyfriend."

John laughs. "Put off all advances or only the unwanted ones?"

"Most of them anyway," she laughs teasingly and looks around. "You are so lucky to be on your own. I can't stand it being back at home."

"What's wrong?" He is concerned for her.

"Everything." Jessica's face tightens. "Let's run away, John," she says. "Let's go somewhere together. I hate being back home. My father is loathsome. He never stops criticising me." She is working herself into a rage. "Keith is horrible, too. What a zombie!" Her eyes are glistening. "Mother lives in a distant dream. It's almost more than I can bear." She grabs John urgently by the shoulders. "Love me, John. Make love to me. Right away."

An hour later, she is more calm, and their conversation resumes. She tells John about how she left the French family where her parents had sent her after only three weeks. "I just picked up my things and disappeared. They were nice, really, Monsieur and Madame. But they were my father's choice, not mine."

"Did you go straight from there to Italy?" John asks.

"Yes. A small town near Florence. I got a job in a cafe, one with a lot of tourists. It suited me just fine. Italy is a lovely country. We must go there together some time."

"What will you do, now that you are back home?"

"Can I come and live with you?" She is half serious.

"Jessica. You must be joking. Your father would have a fit. Anyway, take a look about you. There's barely room for me."

"How is your family?" she asks. "You said your father is sick."

"Yes. Very sick." He explains. "I don't know what Mother will do once he is gone. It is already very difficult for her."

"Do you still love me, John?" she asks.

"More than ever, Jess," he answers. He is sincere. "And you, do you still love me?"

"Yes, I do," she says, taking his hands in hers. "For ever and ever."

33

Since having her little talk at the pub with Sandy Mitchell, Jill had made a few enquiries about Margaret Downie. It seemed to Jill that she could learn a lot from Margaret if she played her cards right, enough to confirm the hypothesis that was gradually forming in her mind as to the full circumstances of Gerald Symons' death.

Margaret was apparently alive and well, and living up in the hills near Tarland. She was now in her sixties. She lived with a man who dealt in antiques. Together they ran a small business selling antique furniture and furnishings out of a restored farm building next to their house. The business was called Burnside Antiques, and the man's name was Edwin Forsyth. That was about all Jill knew when she set out one windy morning on the road to Tarland, some forty miles away.

When Burnside Antiques came into view, it did not appear prepossessing. The grass lawn in front of the house was full of weeds, and the metal sign announcing the business at the roadside was rusting badly. A rather old pale blue Ford was parked carelessly beside the house and there was washing hanging from the clothesline behind. The wind was terrible, and it was a wonder that those sheets and pillowcases didn't all take flight. They looked like they had been on the line for the last week.

Jill pulled up beside the Ford and rang a bell at the front of the house. A woman wrapped in a faded pink dressing gown eventually appeared and stared at Jill. "Are you looking for Edwin?" she asked.

Jill tried to look like your average antique shopper. "Actually, I was hoping to find one or two pieces of furniture."

"I see," was the reply. "We're not really open right now. What exactly are you needing?"

"Have you any side tables, chairs or chests of drawers?"

"Yes. One or two. Please wait a moment and I'll take you around to have a look."

The door closed in Jill's face, so she walked over to the building housing the shop and pretended to take an interest in what appeared in one of the windows. Five minutes later, a man came out of the house followed by the woman, who by now was dressed in blue jeans and a black sweater. The man unlocked the door of the shop and turned on the lights. A miscellany of wooden furniture of varying age and quality was crammed into the small space available. "Have a look," he said.

"This is a wonderful spot for an antique store!" exclaimed Jill. "The views from up here are marvellous. Have you been here for a long time?"

"Almost thirty years," the woman said.

"Thirty-two," the man corrected her. "In any event, thirty-two in my case."

Jill started inspecting the merchandise as the two hovered nearby. "I don't really have a preconceived notion of what kind of piece I'm looking for," she said. "Just something that I really like, something irresistible. Antiques down around Ellon, where I live, are hard to find and the prices are just out of sight."

"There used to be a very good antique store in Ellon," said

the woman. "Not far from the bridge."

"Do you mean the one beside the Post Office?" asked Jill. "If so, it's still there."

"Yes. Beside the Post Office."

"You know Ellon then. Did you once live there?"

"Margaret was born and bred in Tarland," interrupted the man rather roughly. The woman looked annoyed.

"I once lived near Ellon. On Ardeath estate," she said to Jill with a hint of pride.

"I know where you mean," said Jill. "That's very pretty country with those rolling hills and the little village with its pond. Do you remember the pond?"

The man was getting impatient. "Do you see anything you like?" he asked Jill.

Jill pressed on. "I have actually met Keith Symons, who owns Ardeath. He seems like a reasonable man. Was he the laird when you were there?"

The woman made a face. "No, it was his father, Gerald. I knew the son too, but not as much."

"Wasn't the father involved in a gun accident, or something like that?"

The man interrupted a second time. "Margaret was back here in Tarland when that happened."

The two were on the verge of quarrelling, and Margaret in particular was looking annoyed. "No, I wasn't. It was before I moved back. Then you and I joined forces and we set up this business."

"Joined forces, did we," said the man. "What do you know about antiques?"

"That if you don't have the money, you can't buy the inventory," was the sharp rejoinder.

"You were damned lucky. You hadn't a roof over your head."

"Yes, but I did have thirty thousand pounds." Now, Margaret was really angry.

"You could have had even more if you had used your brains."

"There wasn't more to be had. At any rate, not right away. I had to wait. But then..."

Jill was pretending not to show too much interest, but the two suddenly stopped anyway. Then Jill had a stroke of luck. The man's cellphone rang, and he went outside to take the call, leaving Jill alone with Margaret.

"You were very close to Gerald Symons, weren't you," Jill said to Margaret.

"Yes, I was," she replied, giving a quick look at the door to make sure that they were alone.

"Was he an honest man to be in business with?"

Margaret looked startled. How was it that her visitor knew so much? "Yes," she said. "Things were fine, I guess."

"What went wrong?" There was a long silence.

"I loved Gerald," Margaret then said in a rush. "I really did. And I'm sure he loved me as well. But first there was that awful night when the police came. Then Gerald started going with the other girl, and we had a terrible fight. I don't like being double crossed. I was furious. I thought of telling everything to the police. Gerald was terrified that I would do so. He was afraid there would be a scandal. He started giving me money. I would have got more, but then he died. That's when I came back to Tarland and joined up with this imbecile."

Fortunately, the imbecile was still outside on his cellphone.

"How much did Keith know?" Jill asked.

"Keith pretty well stayed out of it. He put through Gerald's last payment, that's all."

"For how much?"

"Twelve thousand."

Jill thanked Margaret and walked back to her car. She was elated. She now had a clear picture of Gerald's life before he died, almost certainly by his own hand for reasons of shame and remorse. She now even had Keith in the net. The only remaining question in her mind was whether the other members of the family knew the facts, and whether any of them had advance warning that Gerald intended to commit suicide.

34

Jessica took up some roses, closed shop and drove off to Mary's house.

She had to speak to John again. She still had a glimmer of hope that they might once more become reunited, if only for a short while. It had now become an obsession. She craved companionship, sympathy, and love, John's love. Without these, she felt she would not be able to cope; she wouldn't make it. She would simply break down.

"Perhaps I'm beginning to go a little mad," she thought. Literally. It was a bit the same feeling that she had felt thirty years ago when John had left her. The more she felt it, the more it made her desperate.

When she arrived at Mary's, John was out in the street with a bucket and rag, removing some particularly muddy spots from his car. "Jessica!" he exclaimed, staring at her apprehensively as she descended from her van.

John's mind was numb as he led her into the house. He was anxious and upset. "Jess," he pleaded. "Please let's be reasonable."

Her heart pounding with anxiety, she handed him the roses. "They're for you," she said. Her voice sounded strange in her ears. Tears started to come and she was unable to hold them back. Her face twisted away so that John couldn't see. Then she completely lost control, and throwing herself on his shoulder, started to cry her heart out.

They remained several minutes in the front hall of the house, her face buried in his shoulder. She occasionally looked up, wanting to see some change in his expression, but his eyes were averted and his lips were firmly shut together, even as his mind was in turmoil. She gradually lost hope.

She suddenly took a step back and stared at him. Her eyes were now full of an anger which bordered on hatred. "I'll leave you alone then, John. I'll get out of your hair." She started to leave, but then turned back. "To hell with you! You go your way, and I'll go mine."

John started to say something, but she was gone, stumbling blindly out of the house and slamming the front door violently behind her.

As Jessica drove away, the reality of her situation started to sink in. She needed to gather her thoughts, to see clearly where she now stood. She pulled over on the side of the road and calmed herself down as best she could. What was she to do? It suddenly came to her that there was only one person who could help her. She reached for her cellphone.

35

Twenty minutes later, Jessica rang the bell at her mother's front door. "Hello, Mum," she said. She felt awful, even if she did make an effort to smile.

"Hello, darling," said Andrea, alarmed at her daughter's appearance. "You look ill. Is there something wrong?" She led her daughter into the house.

Jessica raised her hand to her forehead as if to rub away a bad dream. "John…" she started to say. She broke into a flood of tears

Andrea took Jessica in her arms and stood there patiently, wanting to give her daughter time to recover. "I see. In fact, I had heard that John was back."

"Yes, he's back. But he is treating me like a total stranger."

Andrea smiled and stroked her daughter's cheek. "It's so good to see you, dear. Let's go sit down. We haven't spoken much to each other for a long while, have we?"

A warm feeling came over Jessica; her mother was so kind, so forgiving. "No. We haven't. It's my fault. I really have shut myself up in my little life with the shop and… Well that's about it, the shop."

"In any event, it is always a joy to see you, to have your

visit. But you know, Jessica," Andrea continued cautiously as she led Jessica into her sitting room, "John may have his reasons. You shouldn't chase after him. If he wants to see you, he will let you know."

Jessica looked defiant. "He would love to see me, but he won't admit it."

"John has been away for half a lifetime. Time marches on. I am sure he has changed a lot from the young man you once knew." They sat down on the settee beside each other.

Jessica nodded her head angrily. "How will I ever know? He refuses to let himself go. He barely says anything."

Andrea started to worry. "Perhaps he is married."

"Yes, he's married." Jessica looked down at her lap. Her voice dropped. "He has a wife and two children."

"Well, that's a very good reason for him to stay clear of you. It's never good when a single woman runs after a married man. It can lead to nothing but trouble."

Jessica looked angrily at her mother. "I know all that, Mum. I'm not running after him. I'm not trying to ruin his marriage. I just want to see him, to spend time with him. That's all."

Andrea's face showed concern. "Jessica! Be realistic. One thing can lead to another. Perhaps John himself isn't confident that he can control his emotions. Perhaps he wants to play it safe. After all, you may not be married, but he is."

"You may be right, Mum, but I think that deep down, he still loves me." She looked up at her mother. "Anyways, who cares if he's married?"

"Jessica!" Andrea exclaimed. "I'm sure that his wife does, and it would seem that John does as well."

"But why must we only love one person in our lives? Why is it so important? Aren't we all too earnest, too puritanical about it? I think that if you love someone, that's it. You should take advantage of it. And we even make a moral issue of it. Marital fidelity. What nonsense! And what hypocrisy!"

"Hypocrisy, Jess?"

"Yes, hypocrisy. We all believe in remaining faithful, but do we always succeed? How many marriages are there where both husband and wife remain faithful, the whole time? A minority! Tell me Mum, was Father always faithful to you?"

Andrea threw her head back and looked angrily at her daughter. "Jess. You're talking nonsense. And you even ask me about your father! Why should I answer?" Old memories came flooding back to her. Painful memories. She preferred not to answer.

"Well, I'll answer," Jessica continued. "No, he wasn't. We all knew that. We knew how much he was seeing Margaret Downie. Presumably, they spent much of their time in bed together. That's being pretty unfaithful, I should think."

"It's difficult to think otherwise," Andrea said angrily. She paused. "I knew what was going on, of course. It was plain to see. And I'll tell you right away, Jessica, I wasn't happy about it."

"And what about you, Mum? Were you ever unfaithful?"

"Jessica! That's enough!" Andrea was indignant. Why should she permit herself to be cross-examined like that? "It's none of your business. In any case, what has that got to do with John?"

"I'm not sure. I suppose I would like to think that even if during his visit, he and I were to see each other, were to remember old times, spend time together, that would not be the end of the world."

"It depends on what you mean."

"Perhaps if John and I did relive for a few days the emotions which we once shared, the result would not be the end of his marriage. At the end we could tear ourselves apart and John could return to Labrador and to his wife and family. Meantime, we would have shared a wonderful experience, and isn't that what we should do in our lives, live it to the full?"

"It would be playing with fire. Things might spiral out of

control. John's marriage might be destroyed. Surely, Jess, you wouldn't wish to do that?"

Jessica looked sullen and defiant. Perhaps she did, perhaps she didn't. It depended as much on John as on her. "In any event, it's all academic now. I've done with John. For good."

Andrea was surprised. "What are you saying Jess?"

"Just that. I couldn't take it anymore, so I told him in so many words to get out of my life. I've finished with him. Period."

"Was that just now?"

"Yes, it was. Just before I came over to see you." Jessica looked devastated.

Andrea was worried for her daughter but said nothing. There was nothing more to say. She leaned over to her daughter and gave her a kiss. "Calm down, Jess. It will all settle down, you'll see."

"Do you know whom I met the other day?" Andrea sought to change the subject. "A woman named Jill, who lives on Ardeath with Sylvia Cowan. I liked Jill a lot. She bought a painting from me to give to Sylvia. Isn't it a small world?"

"I know all about them. I've even spoken to Jill on the phone. She ordered flowers for Mary Cowan." Jessica turned to her mother. "I got a fair price from her for the flowers. How much did you get for the painting?"

"Two hundred pounds. It's not a lot, is it?"

"Mum. You're crazy. You can't live like that. You'll starve! You should have asked for a thousand pounds."

"But then she probably wouldn't have bought it. Earning your living as an artist isn't obvious."

"Neither is selling flowers. I stagger on, but I'm never very far ahead of the next bill. If I look at my situation coldly, I have to admit that I'm gradually getting poorer and poorer. I suppose the penny will drop someday."

"That's terrible, Jessica. I'm very sorry for you. These

days, it's not easy to be a single woman."

"We should put the screws on Keith, Mum. It is grossly unfair that he lives on the estate in total luxury while we have to struggle to make both ends meet. Talk about being unfaithful! He receives all that wealth from Father and never lifts a finger to help his own mother and sister. Arguably, he avoids us. That's a whole lot worse than sharing a bit of physical and emotional pleasure with someone other than one's wife!"

"Jessica! What a comparison!" Andrea frowned. "There may be an element of truth to what you say, but I think that you're mixing apples with oranges."

"Even if I am, I think we should go to see Keith together and insist on our rights."

"Insist on our rights?" Andrea asked.

"Yes. Our rights. These are difficult times we're going through. The pandemic. My shop. Your life here. Let's stay together, Mum, you and I. And let's go see Keith, get him to help us out a bit. I'm going to call him tonight and arrange for us to visit him tomorrow. We should have a good chat, the three of us. Without Georgie, I should think. Mum! That's what we're going to do!"

"Just don't bring up your father's death."

"No, I won't, I promise. I'll call you tonight."

36

Keith and Georgie sat finishing their coffee in the dining room of the big house. Keith looked at his watch, not for the first time that morning. "It's almost time. She said they would be here at ten. Do you wish me to see them alone or would you like to join us?"

"I don't mind. Why do you think they are coming?"

"Jessica wouldn't say. It's very unusual, though, she and mother coming out together. I wasn't even aware that they were seeing much of each other. Nor have I seen either of them for quite a while."

"Could it have something to do with John's being back?"

"I can't see any connection. We'll just have to wait to find out."

"In any event, I think I'll excuse myself, and leave the three of you to your own devices." Georgie rose and left the room.

The more he thought about it, the more Keith was convinced that John might have something to do with it. John was some four or five years older than him, so that at school, they had had little to do with each other. There was however one incident involving the two of them which Keith would never forgive or forget.

When Keith was about twelve, he had stayed on in the village after school one day and entered the little shop which sold stationery, newspapers, sweets and sundries. When the lady who kept the shop was looking the other way, he pocketed two chocolate bars and left without paying.

John was nearby and saw what had happened. "Come on, Keith," he had said. "I saw what you did. That's not honest of you." Keith had blushed a deep red.

Some other boys were there and could hear everything. "Keith," said John, "you should either pay for them or return them to the shop." There had followed a general discussion as to what Keith should do. Keith was mortified, and fled home without paying.

Keith now asked himself whether John might again be about to make his life miserable. Perhaps John had returned to Scotland in order to revive his relationship with Jessica. Together, they might attempt to force Keith to make provision for Jessica.

Worse still, they might seek to reopen Keith's father's will and coerce Keith into giving Jessica some part of the inheritance. Keith didn't know the ins and outs of Scottish inheritance law, but he did know that he had received ninety-five percent of what his father had left upon his death. It didn't make sense that you could challenge the division of an estate thirty years after it had opened. However, Jessica could be a formidable adversary.

Furthermore, if any trouble was brewing between brother and sister, their mother would almost certainly take Jessica's side. "Women are like that," he thought. "They're insecure, and whenever an issue comes up, they side with each other no matter what's at stake."

"What was the estate worth?" Keith wondered to himself. Good agricultural land was very much in demand these days. On the other hand, his land was encumbered by leases and under Scots law, tenants enjoyed a strong position. For this reason, tenanted land was far less valuable than land in possession. Even so, the overall value of the estate could run to several millions. Could Jessica, abetted by John, make some claim to a portion of that? If so, it would ruin Keith. He had land, yes, but very little money.

He concluded that he had better be very careful with his visitors. Almost certainly, they had come to discuss money. If not that, what else? He glanced out the window and there they were.

Andrea and Jessica parked on the gravel in front of the house and walked up the wide stone steps leading to the portico. At the front door, they pulled on a chain that set a string of brass bells ringing inside the house. Neither had been back for a long time. They both felt like strangers, strangers ringing at the door of their own home. Keith opened the door to welcome them and tried to do so warmly, although his heart just wasn't in it.

"Hello, Mother. You're looking well as always, and you, Jessica, as beautiful as ever."

"And how are you, dear?" Andrea replied. "Have you got over that arthritis that was troubling you?"

"It still bothers me from time to time, especially when the weather becomes humid. They say that wearing a copper bracelet can help. Have you ever heard of that?"

"No, but I've never been much good at things medical. My mind just goes blank. Where do you want us to go?"

"Let's sit down in the dining room. I lit a fire in there this morning and it should be quite cozy."

"That's kind of you. Lead on and we shall follow."

"Georgie is busy upstairs, but sends you kisses. She put some coffee out for us."

The three went into the dining room, served themselves to coffee and sat down around the big table. There followed a silence, in lieu of conversation.

"It's very good of the two of you to come out for a visit," said Keith, eventually. "Whose idea was it? Yours, Jessica?"

"Yes, in fact, Keith," said Jessica casually. "I have been worrying about Mother. It seems to me that you and I aren't taking enough care of her." This came as a bit of a surprise to Andrea, but she decided to let Jessica handle matters her own way.

"Do you need us to do something in particular, Mother?" asked Keith. "I would naturally be happy to do whatever is possible."

Jessica broke in. "Mum needs a bit of help, Keith. She lives all alone. She has a bit of savings, but not much. She certainly doesn't make much by her painting. Do you know how much she gets for a painting?"

Keith could see the lie of the land. "Surely she receives a good pension from the state. She owns her house. Outright, I believe. Are things that difficult, Mother?"

"No, I get by," was the answer. "In fact, I sold a painting recently and do you know to whom? To one of your tenants, Jill, Sylvia Cowan's friend. Isn't that nice?"

Keith tilted back his chair, his head falling to one side. He made a theatrical grimace. "It's none of my business to whom you sell a painting, Mother, but you should know that Sylvia Cowan is not one of my favourite tenants, and as for Jill, if that's her name, I think she looks like a bit of a tramp."

Jessica saw nothing to gain by remaining diplomatic. Her feelings towards men were exacerbated by her recent dealings with John. She passed to the attack. "Mother just manages, Keith, by selling her paintings. Whereas here, you and Georgie live like kings. You have servants, tenants, silver on the table, portraits on the wall, all of that. Do you think it's fair?"

Keith pretended indifference. "It's merely the life we lead, Jessica. We all lead different lives. Father passed the estate on to me. I had no choice in the matter. In a sense, I am only a custodian of the estate. My duty is to run it efficiently and to keep it together. I have a sort of role that I must play, almost like an actor. The role of the laird. In a sense, I replicate what previous generations of Symons," — here he paused to wave his hand towards the portraits on the walls — "what previous generations of Symons have done before me."

Jessica pointed a finger at Keith accusingly. "Do you call selling off plots of land in the village keeping the estate together?"

Keith blushed with anger. "It costs money to run an estate. Money doesn't grow on trees, you know." This was a favourite expression of his. "I think that Father was very careful in making his dispositions for the estate and for his heirs, and that it's not for us to carp or criticise."

"Very careful, my eye!" Jessica glared at her brother. "Do you call giving thirty thousand to Margaret Downie very careful? Do you think that that's what should have happened to your own mother?"

"That's just a rumour, and if the only reason why you have come out today is to pick a quarrel, you can return to Aberdeen right away. What about the life you have led? It's an embarrassment to us all."

"I work for a living. That's more than you have ever done. You just sit around like a vegetable collecting rents, shooting pheasants and playing cards."

Keith bounded to his feet. "Get out of here!" he shouted. He then realised that he was also ordering his mother out of the house and sat down again. "Unless you can keep a civil tongue."

Their mother intervened, hoping to restore peace. "Keith, I do think that you have a role to play as head of the family. That's what a person in your position should do. You should make sure that Jessica and I are comfortable and reasonably provided for."

"But Mother, until now I had no reason to think that you were not reasonably provided for. We haven't even seen each other, you and I, for well over a year. I haven't seen Jessica for Lord knows how long. What's this all about? Why have you suddenly come out here with these ideas in your minds? I must also say that your timing couldn't be worse. It just so happens that these are very hard times for an estate like this. Shooting revenues are down, rents are hard to collect and yet the expenses continue to mount."

Jessica returned maliciously to the fray. "Why don't you just sell the estate then? It would fetch enough for the three of us to be happy. There is no need for you to continue this strenuous life of yours. You have no children to pass the estate on to. You could retire with your share of the proceeds to the Riviera and spend it all."

This time, Keith was livid. "Since when do you have the right to tell me what to do? Or to pretend to have any financial claim on the estate? It's mine, not yours. Mine alone. Really! If I had known that you were coming out here to make this kind of trouble, I would never have agreed to see you."

"What are you going to do about the estate in your will, dear?" asked Andrea, surprised at her own effrontery. In a sense, it was not at all her business.

Keith looked astonished. "Mother. I really can't answer. Surely, however, one's will is something that is very personal. Particularly as regards one's house."

"We were all once resident in this house," said Jessica. "This is the house I was brought up in. This is the house where Mother was lady of the house for a good number of years. Until you shifted us both out."

Keith got up. "Get out of here," he said to Jessica. "Get out, before I throw you out." Having said that, he left the room.

Jessica and Andrea looked silently at each other, rose from the table, and went out of the room. The meeting was over.

"Was Father any better?" Jessica asked her mother as they drove off.

Andrea was lost in thought. "Yes, of course he was," she said, almost absentmindedly. She was thinking about Keith. She had never appreciated just how self-centred he was. Had he always been that way? It was true what Jessica had said about Keith's shifting them both out of the house. Could it be that Keith had wanted the estate so badly that he had had something to do with Gerald's death?

As some rumours suggested?

Jessica broke the silence. "I hate that man. He's not got a drop of red blood in his veins. I think that when I get home, I'm just going to break down and cry."

37

"Good morning, John." It was Duncan on the telephone.

"Duncan!" John replied. "What's on your mind?" He was still smarting from his recent encounter with Jessica. Why wouldn't she look at it from his point of view? Why did he constantly have to feel guilty?

"I'm going north today for a further meeting with Gordon. We still have one or two matters to resolve. How about joining me? That way, you could meet him and the boys and have a look at the boat. She's at the engineer's in Peterhead having her engines looked at."

"That sounds like a great idea," answered John. "Yes, an excellent idea. It's a bit stifling staying here with Mum all day; I could do with a change. Will you still be negotiating? I don't think I should be with you for that part."

"No. I think you're right there. However, you could meet them and see the boat."

"I tell you what," said John. "Let's go independently. That way, I can do a bit of sightseeing. I had been thinking about going to see the Bullers o' Buchan. I can do so on the way."

Duncan's meeting was at three in the afternoon. He expected to finish at about six and suggested that John meet him in Peterhead harbour at six. So, on that day, John left his mother's house after lunch and set out for the Bullers o' Buchan.

The Bullers were a natural beauty spot on the Buchan coast, just south of Peterhead. At this point, the land fell away to the sea in abrupt high red granite cliffs, and a curious effect of erosion had created a hole some twenty metres wide and thirty-five metres deep in the land next to the cliffs. At the bottom of this great cavity was the sea itself, which rushed in and ebbed out through a short tunnel leading in from the open sea. It was a spectacular sight, enhanced by the sound which the crashing waves made as they swept into the hole and then returned to the seas outside.

When John parked his car in the lot next to the Bullers, there was nobody else; he had the whole place to himself. It was as he had remembered. Around the circular cliffs within the hole were innumerable ledges, crowded with seabirds. There were at least ten species of bird, including kittiwake gulls, cormorants, fulmars and puffins, and in the waters below, two grey seals could be seen swimming about and diving for their dinner. It was a wild and beautiful place. He suddenly thought of home.

"I wish Melba and the children were here," he said to himself. "They would really like this place."

John was beginning to miss his house and family, the North Atlantic's broad emptiness, the sombre skylines of mountain and black spruce, the constant rumour of the river.

Labrador suited him. A man could make his own choices, without being obliged to fall into a particular mould. It was a healthy life, physically and morally, and everyone was your friend, everyone depended on their neighbour. It was a society of *us*, not *me*. This, above all, was very important to John. He felt sorry for people who thought mainly about themselves and failed to take an interest in others.

He thought again about Jessica, about the battering he

had received at their last meeting. Perhaps it was best that way. By sending him packing, she had severed their ties. He now felt freed of the relationship, free to get on with the life which he had chosen for himself. That was a great relief.

Returning to his car, he drove the short distance further north to Peterhead and to its large circular anchorage. To one side was the harbour and at its wharfs, numerous fishing boats. Next to them was the industrial zone, and it was here that he found the engineering facility and moored alongside, the *Sunset Sea*.

He parked next to an office building, went inside, and spoke to a receptionist.

"Mr Christie? Yes, he's here in the boardroom with several other gentlemen. Who can I say is here to see him?"

"His nephew John."

She looked at him with interest. She had noticed his accent. "Are you from Canada then?"

"Yes," said John with a smile.

"I have a cousin living in Toronto, John Gill."

John laughed. "I don't know him, but Canada's a big place."

"Yes, I suppose so. I must go there for a visit some day. One moment please, I'll go tell Mr Christie that you're here."

She disappeared, and shortly afterwards, his uncle and cousins came out of the boardroom with Duncan and a sort of family reunion took place. At Gordon's request, his son Jim then took John off to visit the boat.

"Have you been on a fishing boat before?" Jim asked John as they boarded the *Sunset Sea*.

"Yes, in Labrador," John said. "We have longliners there. I think they're of lighter construction. This boat feels a lot heavier, and it's probably much more powerful and seaworthy."

John was thinking of Duncan. What a great idea it would be for him to invest in the boat. John had noticed how much his brother seemed to enjoy the outdoors when he was visiting Labrador and felt that life as a commercial fisherman would suit Duncan very well.

"This is where we store the fish," Jim explained in his pleasant brogue, pointing out some hatches leading below "and those winches there are for the nets. It's heavy work when the catch comes in and the fishing's good. Duncan may have a surprise or two coming to him," he said with a grin.

"Let's go downstairs," said John. "I'd like to see the galley."

Jim showed him the way, and John imagined Duncan bouncing about in one of those bunks two hundred miles offshore in a North Sea gale. "Rather him than me," he thought happily.

When the two returned to the office building, the others came out of their meeting.

"John," said Duncan. "Gordon brought down several boxes of frozen fish for Mum and for Sylvia. There's one for me as well. They're all in my car."

"That's very generous of you," said John to his uncle. "I'm sure they'll be greatly appreciated."

"It's always easy to be generous," said Gordon, "and I know of no better way to be happy!"

"We still have a few points to cover," continued Duncan. "Would you mind taking the fish to Sylvia and to Mum? There are two boxes for Sylvia. The other three can go into Mum's freezer, and I'll come by and take my share tomorrow. You may as well take my car and we'll switch back tomorrow."

John agreed, said goodbye to Gordon and the boys, and went out to find Duncan's car in the parking lot. He then headed south for Ellon.

By now, the road had become more familiar, and he recognised a number of places along the way. There was the Boddam power station, originally built to be oil fired and later converted to natural gas. Then the turn off to the Bullers, and beyond that, the one to Cruden Bay and the nearby ruins of Slains castle. He recalled that Cruden Bay was the site of a battle at the beginning of the eleventh century, when the Scots under King Malcolm had defeated an invading force of Danes.

Soon, John reached Ellon, where the Ythan river marks the southern boundary of the lands of Buchan. He turned inland, and after twenty minutes, arrived at Ardeath. When he parked in front of Sylvia's cottage, the house appeared deserted, so he walked around to the rear to look for his sister there.

Here he was met by a swarm of bees, all flying around in circles outside the large sliding glass door that led from Sylvia's kitchen onto the patio. Through the glass door, he could see Sylvia and Jill prancing about barefoot and laughing their heads off. At first, he couldn't understand what they were doing, but then he realised that they were extracting honey. He knocked on the glass door and they stopped and stared out at him.

"Come on in," shouted Sylvia, licking the fingers of one hand and making a gesture with the other to show that she was covered with honey and that John would have to open the door himself. "Make it fast," she shouted through the glass, "or the bees will get in."

He raised his index finger to say "one moment" and returned to the car to get two boxes of frozen fish. They were a good weight. "The fishing must be good," he thought to himself.

He managed to open the door, squeeze inside with the fish, and close the door again without letting too many bees into the house. "You two are having fun," he laughed.

They were in jeans and T-shirts, and hard at it. Sylvia held an electric knife in one hand. Her job was to take a frame of honey and, with the heat of the knife, remove the outer covering of wax with which the bees had capped the cells containing the honey. When one side of the frame was uncapped, she would turn the glistening frame around and do the other side. She would then pass the frame dripping with honey over to Jill, who was standing next to a centrifuge which looked like a converted refuse bin and which could take two frames at a time.

"What's in the boxes?"

"Fish. A present from Gordon."

"How wonderful! Is it frozen?"

"For sure."

"Could you put it in the freezer over there for me? I'm too sticky." John complied.

"Explain to me what you're doing."

"Well, we removed the frames, about twenty of them, from the hives three weeks ago. We left them to cure in a cool place. Extracting the honey takes us about three hours and, as you can see, it's a sticky business. It feels like there's honey everywhere, so keep your distance! I prepare the frames and Jill does the extraction. When she's finished, she takes the empty frames outside, and leaves them beside the hives, and the bees clean them up so we can put them away for the winter."

She handed the frame, which she was now finishing, to Jill, who put it into one of the two baskets of the centrifuge. The other basket already held a frame. Jill covered the centrifuge and started turning the crank. You could hear the honey spattering on the inside walls of the centrifuge. John watched Jill admiringly as she leaned over towards him and turned the crank. She noticed and turned her back, still cranking furiously. "It's getting hard to turn. We had better fill some pots."

Sylvia put her knife down, and together, the two lifted the centrifuge up onto a kitchen chair. While Jill tilted it forward, Sylvia opened a spigot at the bottom and filled two white plastic pails with a beautiful golden honey before closing the spigot again. "We don't bother filtering it, so there may be one or two wings or legs in there as well, but they float to the top and are easily removed later on."

John noticed that there were already six or seven pots filled with honey and standing to one side. "How much honey is there in one of those pots?"

"Two kilos. On average, each frame gives us about that much honey, so this year, we are on course to produce thirty-five to forty kilos of honey. Open your mouth." Sylvia picked up a bit of wax saturated with honey that had fallen off her knife. John obeyed and she popped it in his mouth. "Pretty good, don't you think?"

"Mmm."

"But tell me, how did Duncan make out with Gordon?"

John chewed the wax for a short while, getting all the honey out of it, and then removed it from his mouth. "It seemed as if they were doing fine, but I didn't join them in the meeting. I went to visit the boat. I also stopped at the Bullers for a quick visit."

"I haven't been to the Bullers for ages. They are always worth a visit. We must go there one day Jill."

The two got back to work. Jill picked up two empty frames and John opened the door for her as she made a dash outside to leave them by the hive. "I think I'll leave you now, Syl. I had better call Mum. She will be holding dinner for me." He called his mother. "I see. I'll call her tomorrow. Thanks, Mum. I'll be there in thirty minutes."

He turned back to Sylvia. "I'm off. Jessica was looking for me this afternoon. Mum told her I was up north with Duncan. Sorry to leave you with all this mess."

"That's fine. We're almost finished. Give Mum my love, and thanks for the visit and for the fish."

John said goodbye to the two and returned to the car. It was beginning to get dark outside.

When he reached his mother's house, it was dark. He picked up the three fish boxes and brought them to the front door. His mother appeared in the doorway. She had seen him arrive. "What's that?"

"Present from your brother. I hope you have a big freezer."

They opened the boxes on the kitchen table. Inside there were filets of white fish of various kinds, vacuum packed and frozen, each neatly labelled as to its contents. "What a present! Now help me put it all into the freezer."

"One box is for Duncan. He will be coming by tomorrow to fetch it."

"There's enough for all of us and more. Let's go have our dinner."

38

Duncan parted company with Gordon and his sons on the best of terms. The meeting had been thorough, all points had been covered and although there remained a bit of haggling to be done over the price, agreement had been reached on all of the other points. One key element was that of personal relationships. Duncan knew his uncle Gordon well and had always found him very friendly. Now, Duncan felt that he was getting to know his two cousins Bill and Jim a little better. They seemed to him to be energetic, straightforward and reliable. They would make him excellent partners.

He walked across the parking lot in the growing darkness, looking for John's car. Now he would call the estate agent and put his house on the market. His was a good location, and he had never failed to maintain the house in good order. It shouldn't be difficult to sell it quickly, and at a good price.

Living in Fraserburgh would be different. In the Broch, people were predominantly of the fishing community, whereas Aberdeen had long ago become cosmopolitan, with its university, its hospitals, Dyce airport and, of course, offshore oil and gas. The River Dee running inland from Aberdeen was arguably the most fashionable part of Scotland; it was Royal

Deeside, home to the queen at Balmoral and so forth. But the Broch would be fine. He decided he would start off by renting something in Fraserburgh itself, or possibly in the nearby countryside, which was very beautiful.

He thought of how satisfying it had been to bring John back home to see their mother and what a trip that had been for him! He would never forget the beauty of Labrador itself, and the extraordinary characters whom he had met, Charlie, Uncle Joe and, of course, Melba and the children. How many people did he know who could have handled that little canoe so easily in crossing the river to fetch him off his rock?

He also thought how happy he was to have made amends with Sylvia. She was kind to forgive him as she did, but then she was like that; she was not one to hold a grudge forever.

He drove out of the harbour area on the South Road and left Peterhead behind him. A few drops of rain spattered on his windscreen, a passing shower. This was typical Buchan weather, and he had best get used to it.

The South Road took him up to a roundabout where it met the A-90, which also served as the Peterhead bypass. He joined the A-90 and continued southwards down a twisting hill to Boddam where he passed in front of the power station.

After Boddam, the A-90 started to climb the long gradient leading away to the south along the edge of the cliffs near the Bullers o' Buchan. A sign warned him of roadworks ahead. A few years past, he recalled, a fine herd of highland cattle had occupied the field on the seaward side of this stretch of road, looking very picturesque with their long horns and shaggy coats against the backdrop of the North Sea.

A pair of headlights appeared behind him and he sought to make sure that his own lights were on, as it had started to become fully dark. "Damn!" he said as he fumbled about the dashboard, looking for the switch. His frustration switched to anger as the lights behind him came closer and closer. They were beginning to dazzle him. "Dim your lights, you idiot," he shouted.

He wished the driver behind would hurry up and pass. The headlights were so bright now that they stung his eyes, and he had to lean forward and squint in order to see where he was going.

Ahead of him he could make out the profile of a roadworks sign, standing crookedly at the roadside. He slowed, staring out into the darkness beyond it. He was starting to get nervous.

His hands seemed greasy on the steering wheel and he realised that they were sweating.

The other vehicle now pulled out and came alongside his own. Duncan looked ahead; there was no oncoming traffic. Thank God for that. The other driver was now free to pass. Let him get on with it!

Instead, the other vehicle came so close that Duncan found himself forced to move further to his left, towards the shoulder of the road. He hit his horn and shouted "Move over you bastard!". His heart was beating rapidly and he was beginning to panic.

A moment later, he heard a thud and a crunch of metal as the other driver aggressively slammed his vehicle into Duncan's from the side. Duncan's car shuddered. There was no contest, with his car being the smaller of the two. "That bastard's trying to kill me," he realised.

His car hit the shoulder of the road. It was dark now and he couldn't see where he was heading. He was losing control. Out of the corner of his eye, he could see the other vehicle speeding off into the distance ahead of him.

He held tight to the steering wheel and braked hard. The car began to veer dangerously into the void to its left.

Sweat was now pouring down his forehead and into his eyes. His body was rigid and his arms were aching. He began to swear, although there was nobody there to listen to him. His heart was pounding furiously.

The car hit something hard and, with a violent jerk,

tipped over onto its side and started to slide away from the road. "Jesus," he said out loud, "I'm going to die!" He gripped the steering wheel to steady himself even as the car rocked violently from side to side, and then rolled onto its roof. It skewed wildly, gathering speed as it descended a steep incline leading it to the top of the cliffs. Duncan's head smashed into something hard inside the car and he could feel the blood oozing out through his hair.

His whole life flashed briefly through his mind. School, the army, Ruth, his trip to find John, Labrador. He blacked out.

In another instant, the car was over the edge of the cliffs, its headlights shining down through the darkness to the black waters below.

39

The telephone rang. Mary rose from her chair to answer. "Yes. This is Mary Cowan."

....

"Yes. He is my son."

....

"I beg your pardon. What did you say?" Mary's face went grey as ashes. She sat down again and wordlessly, passing the receiver to John, she closed her eyes and started to rock back and forth in her chair.

After the caller rung off, John hung up the phone and went slowly to his mother's side. He felt sick to his stomach. He put his hand softly on her shoulder.

"Duncan has had a terrible accident, Mum, driving down yesterday evening from Peterhead. I'm afraid he's dead. Apparently he died immediately." He tried hard to control his voice, to fight off his emotion.

"Did he hit another car?" she asked mechanically.

"No, Mum. He went off the road." John sat down heavily, and a great weariness came over him.

They sat there together, neither knowing what to say, neither wanting to break the silence. Finally, Mary said ,"You had better call Sylvia." John rose and went over to the telephone.

"Syl. Duncan had a car accident last night." His voice broke and he waited a moment before being able to continue. "He's dead."

....

"Yes. Dead. I know. It's horrible. Too horrible to believe. We just had a call from the police in Peterhead. Poor Duncan."

....

"On the road just south of Peterhead. Near that lay-by."

....

"The police think that it must have been at around seven-thirty yesterday evening."

....

"They told me that he probably lost control of his car and went off the road. The car went over the cliffs and they had to get the harbour police to fish it out."

....

"You do whatever you think right. I'll just stay here and

take care of Mum. Call us later if you have learned anything more."

40

Jill slowly parked at the Boddam lay-by. Strong gusts of wind were shaking the car and heavy drops of rain were driving against its windscreen. Visibility out to sea was close; they could barely see the grey water with its angry whitecaps rolling in onto the rocks below.

Sylvia was sobbing quietly in the passenger's seat, her right hand held to her forehead, and Jill tried to comfort her. "Do you want me to stay here with you, Syl, or may I go out and have a look?"

"You go. I'll stay here," Sylvia said.

Jill walked back along the road, shielding herself from the rain as best she could and trying to imagine just what might have happened. There was no traffic and she was alone with her thoughts. There were some tyre marks on the wet road which to her untutored eye might have been fresh. However, there were always tyre marks on roads, she thought.

She finally came to where a car had recently gone onto the shoulder of the roadway, and following its marks, she was able to see where it had rolled, where it had slid, and finally where it had gone over the cliffs. This was clearly where Duncan had died.

She had a vision of Duncan, terrified at the wheel of his car, gradually leaving the road, gradually losing control, gradually losing hope, finally tipping over the edge, the car's headlights flashing wildly in the dark, plunging down onto the rocks below. She was shocked. It was too horrible to imagine.

Sylvia's brother had died in this spot, she thought. Duncan! She couldn't change that. She wanted to understand though, to know why. "What do you think happened, Jill?" she asked herself. "What were Duncan's last moments like? Why did he lose control? Have a look around."

The road was straight here and visibility was fine. Duncan could have fallen asleep or swerved to avoid a roe deer. Perhaps he had been drinking.

She walked back and forth through the long grass near the top of the cliff, looking, just looking. Just in case. The skid marks were clearly visible. There were also the usual bits of litter here and there, a paper cup, a plastic spoon. One thing finally caught her eye, one thing that did seem unusual. It was a small bit of red plastic, the kind used for a side light or a taillight, lying off to one side and hidden in some long grass. She left it there, but a nagging thought arose in her mind that it might be of importance.

A second vision now came to her, one of Duncan driving along this stretch of road in the darkness, looking into his rear-view mirror and seeing the bright headlights of a car rapidly gaining on him from behind. She could feel his anger, and then his terror as that car came alongside and crowded him off the road and onto the verge. Then the violent shocks as his car skidded and rolled towards the cliffs, and Duncan's sickening realisation that his life was coming to an end.

Could she be right? Could that be what had happened?

She returned to the car where Sylvia was sitting silently, white as a sheet.

"Syl. Have you your cellphone?"

"Yes."

"I think you should call your uncle Gordon to tell him the news. You might also ask him if Duncan had anything to drink before leaving the others last night."

Sylvia made a great effort and called her uncle.

"He can't believe it, Jill," she said, as she rang off. "He says that Duncan left them in the best of spirits, and that they had nothing to drink. He says that it's a terrible thing to have happened, and that he will visit Mum in the days to come."

As Jill sat there in the car, thinking of Duncan, she was suddenly struck by the parallel between Duncan's death and that of Gerald Symons thirty years previously. Both were violent deaths. Both appeared to be accidental. And in both cases, there were ambiguities. How was it that she, of all people, had become involved? She, who only a few days ago had heard of neither man. Wasn't life strange? It made her wonder if she was living a real life or if she was living in a dream. Sylvia stirred beside her and blew her nose.

"Syl," Jill said gently, taking Sylvia's hand. "I feel very sorry. What would you like us to do? Would you like me to take you to your mother's?"

"Yes, please."

"Let's go. Perhaps you should call her to say that we're on our way. However, I just want to go back there where Duncan went off the road in order to fetch something. I won't take a moment."

Jill got out of the car and, returning to where Duncan's car had crossed over to the top of the cliff, looked for the little bit of red plastic. After a short while, she located it and picked it up. On closer examination, it clearly did come from the side light or the taillight of a car. "Taillights don't break by themselves," she thought. "There may well have been a second vehicle." She returned to join Sylvia and the two of them left for Aberdeen.

They parked near Mary's house and went inside. Mary and John were sitting silently in the living room. Sylvia explained that they had visited the place of Duncan's accident, saying that really, there was nothing to see.

Jill eventually turned to Mary. "Has anyone told Duncan's wife Ruth?" she asked.

"No," said Mary. "John. Will you please do so?" She fidgeted with the hem of her skirt. She was exhausted. "If you will all excuse me, I'm going to my room to lie down."

After a short conversation with Ruth, John hung up. "She says that she is horrified by the news. She says that at the time of the accident, she and her children were at home watching TV."

Jill then turned to John. "Did Duncan ever discuss his affairs at the bank with you?"

John was lost in his thoughts, and slow to respond. "A bit. Why?"

"I suppose they'll find out about Duncan's accident soon enough. However, I'm curious to know if there were any matters that were bothering him when he left his job."

John frowned. He really couldn't see the point of Jill's question. "He did talk about a developer who was giving him a hard time and had even openly threatened him."

"Did that worry him?"

"Do you mean to the extent that the developer might have wished to harm him? No. Duncan's reaction was that having tipped his hand, the developer would be a damn fool to do anything for real."

"Can you think of anything else that Duncan might have had on his mind at the bank?"

John thought for a moment. He was having difficulty thinking about Duncan without thinking of the accident itself, of Duncan's death. "Duncan said he was a bit embarrassed because he had discovered that Keith Symons' wife had money in a tax haven."

"Embarrassed?"

"Yes. He didn't really know what to do, turn a blind eye

or call the Revenue. But surely, Jill, Duncan wasn't murdered. Aren't the police treating the case as an accident? Why these questions?"

"You are right, John. The odds are heavily in favour of its being an accident." At this point, the three fell silent. "He must have fallen asleep or lost concentration for some other reason, hit the shoulder of the road, lost control of his car and left the road completely. It's odd though. That was a good car he was driving. You would have thought that having hit the shoulder, he would have come to his senses and regained control."

John looked at her with an odd expression on his face. "He wasn't driving his car. We exchanged cars in Peterhead so that I could bring back the frozen fish. He was driving my car. My rental car. The little orange Fiat 500."

Jill said nothing for a moment. She was thinking hard. "I see," was all that she eventually said.

Since it seemed unlikely that Mary was going to reappear soon, Sylvia and Jill excused themselves and returned to the car.

They sat in the car for a while without moving. Sylvia fussed with her safety belt, massaged her forehead for a while, collapsed back into her seat and then said wearily, "Tell me, Jill, why all those questions?"

"Syl, I hadn't shown you this before." Jill produced the little piece of red plastic. "I found this in the long grass more or less where Duncan went over the cliff. It must come from a broken taillight or side light."

Sylvia glanced at it. "And so?"

"Jill. I think that it raises the question of whether there was another car involved in the accident. The two cars could have hit each other in some way, and one of them could have lost this piece of plastic."

Sylvia showed little interest. "It was probably there before Duncan's accident," she said.

"Possibly," said Jill, "but it looks very clean. I don't think that it had been there very long before I found it. Let's go home now. You must be exhausted. We should have something to eat." The two drove off in silence.

"Don't you see," said Jill after a while. "Let's imagine Duncan driving along in that little Fiat. A second car hits him slightly from the rear or side, enough to damage the taillight or side light of one car or the other. Surely the other driver would notice. He wouldn't just drive on without having noticed anything."

"Yes," said Sylvia slowly.

"If the other driver noticed the collision, he would certainly also see Duncan's car leaving the road and its headlights flashing as it went over the cliff. In such a case, if it was an accident, he would stop and immediately report the matter to the police."

"Unless it was hit and run."

"Possibly. But let's pursue the alternative. What if the driver of the other car wanted to cause the accident?"

"Hence your questions. Who might have wished to kill Duncan?"

"Not necessarily, Syl," said Jill quietly. "We now know that the car was John's. The question may be different. Who might have wished to kill John?"

41

Sylvia and Jill arrived home at just before six that evening and switched on the radio to catch the news. They listened in silence to the announcement.

The man whose body was found this morning in a car at the foot of the cliffs south of Peterhead has been identified as Duncan Cowan, fifty-one years of age, businessman from Aberdeen. Mr Cowan apparently lost control of his vehicle on the road above at around seven-thirty the previous evening. He was alone at the time of the accident. Any member of the public who may have witnessed anything material is requested to contact the Peterhead police.

That was all. Jill turned off the radio. So now, news of Duncan's death had been made public. They sat there in silence and had a quick bite to eat. Finally, Sylvia spoke.

"Do you really think that someone caused the accident thinking that it was John in the car?"

"I think it's a distinct possibility."

"Why didn't you want to discuss it with John when we

were at Mum's house earlier on?"

"Sylvia. I think that for the time being, you and I alone should go deeper into what may have happened. When we know some of the answers, it will be time enough to share them with the others."

"Jill, you're taking a big responsibility on your shoulders. Duncan was seemingly involved in a road accident. You want to turn it into a murder."

"I'm sorry, Syl. I don't want to turn it into anything. If you insist, I will let the matter drop."

"Anyhow, that piece of plastic. Don't you think that the police would have seen it and picked it up if they had thought it of interest?"

"Our police are overworked and understaffed. It is more than likely that they would not have noticed it." Jill shrugged. "Road accidents happen all the time. The police just don't have the time to investigate them all properly, not even the fatal ones."

"I suppose that's so." Sylvia suppressed a sigh. "Poor Duncan. I just can't stop thinking about him."

Jill looked up at Sylvia. "Syl. Would you have the strength to go out again this evening? There is something that I would like to check."

"Check?"

"Yes. If there was a second car, it may have a broken taillight or a scratch somewhere. It's just a hunch, Syl, but if I don't follow up on it, I'll never be able to forgive myself."

"Where do you want to go?"

"I want to have a look at Jessica's van."

Sylvia gasped. "Jessica?"

"Yes, Jessica. Let's go look first. Afterwards, if we find anything, we can look for an explanation. And if checking out Jessica's van turns nothing up, I want to look at Keith's car. Do you know where Jessica lives?"

"Yes, in Potterton. At the end of the village."

"Has she a garage or does she park out of doors?"

"She has a garage. The house is recent, and the garage is attached to the house."

"Let's leave in thirty minutes. Can we take your car?"

"Of course."

Jill went to change into a black track suit and trainers. She put into her pocket the small light that she usually wore on her forehead when jogging in the winter evenings and picked up two hive tools from amongst Sylvia's beekeeping equipment. "Let's go."

They drove slowly to Potterton, where Sylvia pointed out Jessica's house. Jill had Sylvia park fifty metres away, facing the house. "So you can watch," she said. They sat for twenty minutes or so, talking quietly and waiting for the light outside to fade a bit more. Lights came on in the house; Jessica was at home.

Jill got out of the car and disappeared into the nearby shrubbery. She was feeling nervous. What if she lost her way and ended up in someone's garden? What if a dog barked? She slowly made her way forward, using all possible cover to hide herself from Jessica's view and from that of her neighbours. By the time she arrived at the back of Jessica's garage, it was completely dark outside.

There was a small sash window set in the rear wall of the garage about five feet off the ground. Jill used the hive tools to pry it open and jammed it up as far as it would go. It made a slight squealing noise and for several seconds, she froze. The window was now just open enough for her to fit through and silently, she lay the hive tools on the ground beside her. Grasping the window frame, she gave a small jump and put her head and shoulders through the window. Inside the garage, it was pitch black.

Switching on her headlamp for a moment, she was able to see that within the garage, there was nothing on the floor below the window. She slid through the window, falling silently to the floor within. Her heart was pounding, but so far so good! As long as Jessica didn't hear her!

Jill listened to see if she could hear any sounds coming from the house. Nothing. Groping forward in the darkness, she felt the front of Jessica's van. Putting on her lamp for a moment, she saw that there were no scratches or broken lights at its front. The side of the van nearest to the house came next and yielded the same result. Likewise, the rear of the van. She moved to the fourth side, the side on which a passenger would normally sit.

There was no sign of a broken taillight or side light. However, flashing on her headlamp one more time, she saw a long scratch on the side of the van. She felt her blood pressure rising rapidly. The next question was whether there was any sign of orange paint, paint the colour of the Fiat 500 that Duncan had been driving.

Here, she was disappointed. The side of the van showed only its own colour and that of the logo of Jessica's flower shop. However, there was one area of the scratch that seemed to have been worked on, possibly with sandpaper. She put her light on again and had a quick look around the garage in case she could see any sandpaper.

Just then, she started to hear sounds coming from the house. Jessica was moving about. She had just turned on the TV, or perhaps a radio. Jill decided that she had better get back outside as quickly as possible. As she groped her way back to the window in the darkness, her feet came in contact with a garbage bag. She put her light on briefly and saw that the bag was both open and half full. She grabbed it and pushed it through the window ahead of her. She then made her own exit, closed the window behind her, and picking up the bag and the two hive tools returned slowly through the darkness to the car.

"Jill! You're back. How did it go?" Sylvia asked. "Did you find anything? Did Jessica notice you? I've never been so nervous in my life.”

“I wasn’t very calm myself, Syl. Let’s go home. There is a long scratch on the van, on the passenger side. It could be what we’re looking for.”

They drove home, Jill in silence and Sylvia wishing that Jill would say something and reveal her inner thoughts. Upon their arrival, Jill asked Sylvia to leave the car outside. The two then went into the garage, where Jill turned on the lights and started emptying the garbage bag. After two spent light bulbs, a few discarded boxes and some dirty rags out came two used sheets of sandpaper and on the second one was a clear trace of orange paint, the same colour of orange as the car Duncan had been driving.

They both felt exhausted and went into the living room where Sylvia lit a small fire while Jill fetched two wine glasses and a half empty bottle of cold Pinot Grigio. She also put the two sheets of sandpaper together with the small bit of broken red plastic on the low table in front of the sofa where they sat together side by side.

“Syl. We need to discuss this a bit.”

“I wish we would!”

“I think that what happened to Duncan was no accident. I think that the driver of the other vehicle was Jessica, and that she deliberately pushed Duncan’s car off the road with her van, thinking that John was inside, not Duncan.”

“John, not Duncan.” It seemed so strange, and so unfair. Sylvia had difficulty focussing on what Jill was saying.

“Jessica barely knew Duncan. She had no reason to kill him. She probably hadn’t seen him more than a couple of times over the last thirty years.”

“I suppose that’s so.”

“On the other hand, we know that she and John were very close before he left for Canada. For both of them, it was their first love, and it went on for four or five years. It’s just possible that when John came back here after all those years and she couldn't win him back, she became desperate."

"Yes, John said as much to me the other day."

Jill continued. "Your mother told us that Jessica called earlier yesterday and that she told Jessica that John had gone north to Peterhead and would only be returning to Aberdeen at the end of the day. Perhaps Jessica went up to Peterhead at the end of the afternoon, saw the roadworks on the stretch of road by the Bullers, saw the opportunity to surprise John in that bit of road and lay in waiting for him to appear in his orange Fiat."

"I don't know what to say. Keep going."

Jill nodded. "But there was a mix-up. John wasn't driving the car, Duncan was. And in the darkness, Jessica couldn't see that. She drove alongside the Fiat and forced it off the road. Duncan lost control and that was it."

Sylvia put her hands to her forehead. "My God! What do we do now?"

"At present, only three persons know or may know what happened, the two of us and perhaps Jessica herself. On the other hand, three other people, your mother, John and just possibly Andrea, if she has heard the news, presumably think that Duncan died in an accident."

"It's terrible. If John were to think that Duncan was murdered in his place, he would never forgive himself, not for the rest of his life."

"I also hate to think of the consequences if Andrea was to think that her daughter Jessica had committed murder, and was to be sent to prison for the rest of her life."

"But is this information that we have the right to withhold?"

"Clearly not, but I think that we should talk to Jessica before telling your mother and John. That way we don't run the risk of making a terrible mistake."

42

Jessica hasn't slept or changed clothes since it happened. She has barely eaten. Most of her time she spends in the armchair of her living room by a small fire, trying to calm her nerves. Her heart is pounding. She is like a stag at bay.

When she left the house the previous afternoon, she had intended to make one last attempt to find common ground with John. There had to be a way! So she had driven north, somehow expecting to meet with him, to plead with him, to win him to her point of view.

Somewhere along the way, she had started to compare the lives which the two of them had been living: he with a wife and family, settled, sure of himself. She, with her succession of false starts, a difficult and unhappy existence with at the end nothing much to show for it, reduced to begging from that shit of a brother of hers. This was the bitter reality, and it made her furious.

Then, in the roundabout, she had seen him coming from the opposite direction in the orange Fiat. She had followed the car as it headed south out of Peterhead. God knows what passion overcame her at this moment. She must have gone mad. At first, as she came up behind the Fiat, she thought of ramming it from the rear. At the last moment, she decided not to do so, as she feared that she would lose control of her van. In a blind rage, she stepped hard on the accelerator and swerved out alongside the Fiat. She actually screamed as she sideswiped it. She then sped off into the darkness.

Now she is back at home. She didn't make it to bed last night. She hasn't gone out all day. She has barely moved from her armchair in the living room. She is terrified. "What have I done?" she continually asks herself, running her hand through her hair. Her throat is dry, so she gets up and fetches herself a glass of water in the kitchen.

At one point, she jumps out of her chair. "The van! I wonder if there are any marks on the van." She hopes that there are none, that somehow, the whole thing is just a bad dream. She runs out to the garage to check the van. She almost faints at what she sees: a long scratch along its passenger side and a dirty smudge of orange paint. Mechanically, she picks up some sandpaper, removes the orange paint and returns to the living room.

She turns on the news periodically, but nothing is said about an accident on the road south of Peterhead. The day goes by slowly, ever so slowly. Then comes the devastating news broadcast at six. She can't believe her ears. "Do they know what they're talking about? Is it possible that the Fiat went over the cliff? That John died? Why do they mention Duncan? Did I cause all this? Have they got it right? Am I going mad?"

She gets up and paces aimlessly back and forth. "The Internet! Yes, I can check it on the internet." She does so, and the terrible reality is confirmed. For some reason, Duncan has died. Not John, but Duncan. Now she is truly terrified.

She is dizzy and almost vomits. "I have killed someone, Duncan, whom I can't even remember. Deliberately. It's murder."

"I'm finished. There's no way out."

Tears flood her eyes and for a few minutes, she lets them come. She is overcome by an intense feeling of sorrow. Sorrow for Duncan, sorrow for her life, sorrow for what awaits her. She blacks out.

When she comes to, she starts to think about all the things she is about to forfeit: the blue sky, the stars, birds, flowers, her mother. She is happy to think that she has seen her mother before going. John? No, absolutely not. She is not going to miss John. He is going to miss her!

She gets up and paces about aimlessly. Where did she go wrong? At what point did she take or fail to take decisions that could have altered the course of her life, that could have saved her from this?

Had being so beautiful been a curse? She thinks not. Should she not have had her early love affair with John? No.

What was it then? Perhaps she should never have returned from her year in Italy. Instead, she should have stayed away from home and roamed the world. One couldn't tell where that would have taken her.

Jessica is overcome by the futility of what she has done. She sits there, exhausted. "The letter!" she suddenly says out loud. "I must read it once more."

She stands up and goes into her bedroom. Rummaging in a drawer, she finds what she is looking for: a small, stained envelope with her name on it, written in John's handwriting. She takes it up and, returning to her chair in the living room, removes the letter from its envelope. The paper is worn; she knows the letter by heart, even the places where John has crossed words out and started a word or sentence again. She reads it one last time.

Dearest Jess,

I want you to know that I love you and always have. You are so wonderful, so special.

We both have our lives in front of us. I have been thinking for some time about my future, and I have decided that I don't want to stay in Scotland; I want to make a fresh life in a new world. Tomorrow, I leave for Canada, probably somewhere in the north.

I know that this means that we will part. It is what I wish. Please forgive me.

John.

Jessica rips the letter up slowly and deliberately and throws the pieces in the fire. She turns the radio on. Her time is over.

43

Just after breakfast, the phone rang, and Jill picked up the receiver. She heard a woman's voice. A feeling of alarm came over her as she realised that it was Andrea.

"Jill. Jessica. She's...dead."

"No!" Jill was stunned. She wasn't prepared for this. The train of tragic events simply refused to stop. She was suddenly very worried for Andrea herself.

"Andrea. I'm coming over right away. Don't move!" She hung up and turned to Sylvia. "Syl. Jessica's dead." She rushed out without a further word.

When Jill arrived, Andrea was sitting in her living room in her dressing gown and pyjamas, having a coffee. Her face was red and she held a wet handkerchief to her eyes. "She swallowed pills, Jill, a lot of them, and died of an overdose. A neighbour walking his dog looked in and saw her in a chair. He called the police. Oh, God!" Andrea cried out. "Oh, God!"

"Poor Andrea. I'm so sorry for you." Jill sat beside her and wrapped an arm around her shoulder.

"You didn't know her, Jill, but she was a good girl," Andrea sobbed. "She was very direct, very honest. But impetuous and headstrong as well."

"I wish that I could have known her," said Jill. "I am sure that I would have liked her." She paused. "She was terribly in love with John, wasn't she?"

"Yes, she was. They were lovers for several years before John left for Canada. I think that those must have been the happiest years of her life."

"How are you feeling, Andrea?" Jill was worried for her. "Is there anything I can do?" She picked up a shawl from the sofa next to her and wrapped it around Andrea's shoulders.

"No. Just stay with me for a while." Andrea buried her face in the handkerchief and they sat there together in silence.

Jill started to think about Duncan's death, about Jessica's van and about the sandpaper with its traces of orange paint. And now, Jessica's suicide. The whole tragedy came into focus. "John's return was too much for her," she said, more to herself than to Andrea.

Andrea heard. "I think so. They saw each other several times, but Jessica wanted more than just to see him, to be with him. She tried to push matters too far."

"And he refused."

"Yes." Andrea reflected through her tears. "Love is a powerful force, Jill. When it is shared, it is everything, but if it is withheld, it can lead to tragic consequences."

The two sat together for a long while, each thinking her own thoughts.

Andrea looked intently at Jill. "You are very kind to sit here with me, Jill. Very kind. You can't appreciate just how grateful I am for your support. You are a true friend."

Jill took her hand. "Andrea," she replied. "I have become very attached to you. It is strange. Perhaps it's because you are like the mother that I lost so long ago. Just in part, though. I think that there's also something else as well. I seem to be discovering that I have a basic need to be close to others and if needs be to help them in order to fulfil myself, in order to be happy."

She then added, "Andrea, I also have a confession to make to you. One that will take you back thirty years to another terrible moment in your life. Will you permit me to say what I have in mind?"

Andrea looked surprised. "Of course. What confession?"

"Andrea. I have occasionally written articles for the press. Freelance. A month or so ago, Sylvia mentioned your husband's death to me. She said that it had caused a stir locally and told me how, at the time, it was treated as an accident. I was intrigued and started asking questions. It seemed to me that the affair could be the subject for a new article. I'm not so sure now."

"Why not?"

"Jessica's death. Coming so soon after another tragic death, that of Duncan, Sylvia's brother." Andrea nodded, and Jill continued. "These deaths are too real, too much more important than a mere article. Some things are best left unsaid. Like your secret thoughts and hidden reminiscences."

Andrea almost managed a smile. "You liked that phrase, didn't you? But tell me. What did you unearth about my husband's death? Say what you wish to say. You won't offend me."

Jill felt relieved. "There goes my article," she thought. "I concluded that your husband committed suicide. That he did so because he was ashamed of what he had gotten himself into, and desperate because he had destroyed his marriage and most of his family life."

Andrea couldn't imagine how it was that Jill was telling her all this. There was nothing incorrect in what she was saying. However, did Andrea want to hear all about her husband's shortcomings and about his death, particularly at this time?

"I think that you are right," she said finally, "but that would hardly make interesting reading in any article you might write."

"In any event, be assured," Jill told her. "I won't write it."

Andrea was exhausted but had to ask the question. "What do you mean when you refer to what my husband had gotten himself into?" Jill paused and at first, Andrea said nothing. "Go ahead, Jill," she finally said wearily. "You had just as well tell me."

Jill took a deep breath and continued. "I think that he was running a call girl operation, supplying prostitutes to various customers throughout the countryside."

Andrea nodded. "Margaret Downie being one of them?"

"Yes. In fact, they were doing it in business together."

Andrea shook her head. She was drained emotionally. She put a hand on Jill's shoulder, almost as if she needed her support. "If that's so, and I believe it may well be, then he was better off dying when he did. Jill, you are telling me things that I didn't know, but should have guessed. And yes, I would prefer it if you didn't write that article."

"I won't," Jill promised. "However, there is one thing that I might do, if you have no objection. Your son Keith was aware of this, even if he took no part in it directly. I would like to confront him with the truth."

"You have my blessing," Andrea said. "Go ahead."

That evening, Jill and Sylvia sat next to each other, very close, silently watching the fire and sipping a glass of wine.

"What are we going to do about them?" asked Sylvia, pointing at the piece of red plastic and the two sheets of sandpaper that had remained on the low table in front of the fireplace since the previous day. "Now that Jessica is dead, they don't matter, do they?"

"No, they don't. Let's burn them."

"I agree."

They each threw a sheet of the sandpaper onto the flames and watched the fire flare up while the paper burned. Jill then put the bit of red plastic onto the hot coals, and it melted and burst into flame.

44

Jill stood by expectantly, waiting for a signal from Sandy Mitchell. She was dressed in outdoors gear and wore her wellingtons. The ground where she stood was wet and swampy, but it was a lot worse over where the beaters were slowly gathering. Far ahead of her in the opposite direction she could see men walking out into a field in front of a wood. That would be Keith placing the guns. It was the first Saturday of October and the Ardeath shoot was about to start.

Jill had seen Sandy in the village a few days back, in fact the same day that she and Sylvia saw John off at the airport. He had told her about the shoot and she volunteered to help. "Of course!" Sandy said. "You could be a flanker."

"What's a flanker?" she asked.

He grinned. "It's a cushy job. You walk along ahead of the other beaters, but off to the side. You carry a white flag, and if you see any pheasants running or flying out on your side, instead of heading forward towards the guns, you flap like mad."

Jill had been issued with her white flag, and briefly practised flapping it. It made a convincing noise.

It was a good day, with the west wind showing promise.

Apparently, wind was essential to make the birds fly well.

As she waited for the shoot to start, Jill thought about Sylvia. She had shown a lot of emotion when John had finally left on his return trip to Labrador. After that, however, she had seemed more relaxed.

Events had put a great strain on them all. Jill particularly remembered the conversation which she had had with Andrea. For Jill to abandon writing the article about Gerald's death was a watershed moment. It meant that she was no longer on the outside looking in. She was part of the community now. Writing an exposé about strangers was one thing; writing it about your friends and family was another.

In her mind, the article was still born, but she still wanted to confront Keith with the circumstances of his father's death and have him admit to the role which he had played. For about the tenth time in the past week, she identified in her mind the last pieces of the puzzle.

The last years of Gerald's life, if publicly known, would have brought scandal onto the family. This was why Gerald paid Margaret money to stay quiet. The same feeling of shame that caused him to pay Margaret money would quite logically have led him to commit suicide. Jill therefore assumed that this was what had happened. In any event, she had already discounted in her mind the possibilities of murder and of a shooting accident.

On the day of Gerald's death, Keith decided not to go out shooting with his father after lunch. This was not completely unusual. However, it was also possible that Keith had a reason. It seemed likely that he knew what his father intended, and did not wish to stop him from acting, either on account of some notion of the family's honour or simply because he wanted to inherit the estate right away.

How might Keith have known what his father intended to do? It was possible, indeed highly likely, that Gerald left a suicide note. That way, he could apologise to Andrea for the pain and embarrassment he had caused her. But assuming that he did, where did he leave it? What had happened to it?

Andrea had said that Keith was in the estate office that morning, clearing up some old files. Perhaps that was where he had found a suicide note. Found it, read it and destroyed it.

Jill felt increasingly confident in her analysis and couldn't wait to put it to the test.

Her thoughts were interrupted by a great shout, followed by the distant blast of a horn. The shoot had started. She obeyed Sandy's orders, moving forward along the side of the ground ahead of the beaters, and flapping at anything that moved.

A roe deer, and then a second one, appeared out of nowhere. Cantering forward towards the line of guns and picking their spot, they passed through in safety. The guns had been instructed only to shoot at flying birds.

The occasional wood pigeon came out of the woods and flew over the guns, provoking a volley of shots.

The beaters were now coming closer, and Jill moved quickly forward. Suddenly the beaters shouted in chorus and a great flush of pheasants rose ahead of them. Fifteen or twenty of them passed over the guns and as many doubled back over the heads of the beaters. A lot of shots were fired. Four or five pheasants came Jill's way and she attempted to flap them back into the drive.

When finally the beaters came close to the line of guns, Keith sounded his horn and his guests all unloaded. The beaters' dogs arrived and started to dash about, some looking for birds and others carrying birds back to their masters. Amongst them was Jock, who had been stationed behind the guns with his dog and was picking the birds as they fell. This was the part which Jill enjoyed the most, seeing the dogs work, their masters cursing when two dogs tried to carry the same bird, the whole a scene of movement and confusion that had been enacted like this in Scotland for decades, even centuries.

The first drive yielded twenty-seven birds picked and the men all proceeded to the second drive. This time it was a short drive, a small field of turnips, and all were asked to stay very quiet so as not to disturb the birds. The drive proved to be a good one with a number of very high pheasant, and also a covey of partridge, of which two were shot.

The third drive was through a mossy wood of beech and sycamore, the guns encircling it in fields of barley stubble on two sides. There were a few high-flying pigeon that jinked to left and right as soon as they saw a gun being raised, and the guns enjoyed themselves, laughing at all the shots that they took and missed. The wood yielded few pheasant, however.

The fourth drive was down a long belt of trees, with thick brambles underneath and swampy ground to one side. By now, the pheasants had had plenty of time to wander out. Also, the drives had been planned so that birds shifted in the first three drives would find themselves in the fourth drive, in that belt of trees. Jill could see them running back and forth under the trees and knew that she would be busy. She was.

Time and again the birds came flying forward in twos and threes, hurtling down the belt just over the treetops. A number of them curled away to her side and she succeeded in coaxing a few back over the woods. Sometimes the guns found a shot difficult because of the branches, but the birds were great and the drive was clearly going to be by far the best of the day. It took the beaters and dogs a full half-hour to pick up after the drive.

They did a short but productive fifth drive before lunch and broke off for sandwiches at the kennels, the guns to one side and the beaters to another.

Jill's feet were sore, and she removed her boots as she sat under a tree with a thermos of hot soup.

Three more drives followed after lunch, and then it was time to stop as the birds were to be allowed to return to their roosts for the night, and, in any event, it was beginning to get dark. The guests went back to their vehicles, and the ritual of removing boots, setting out and counting the bag, passing around the cherry brandy, tipping Mitchell and thanking Keith took place. The beaters started drifting off to the pub in the village.

Keith was off to one side and his gun was still over the crook of his right arm when Jill came up to him. He had not realised that she had spent the day with the beaters, acting as a flanker.

Jill had changed out of her wellingtons and barbour, and was lightly dressed and wearing trainers. "Good afternoon, Mr Symons. That was a successful day's shoot."

"Good afternoon. Were you beating?"

"Yes, I was one of the flankers." Keith turned as if to head back to the big house. "I was very sorry to hear about your sister," Jill said.

"That's good of you. Thank you. Excuse me now, I must go."

Jill was not to be deterred. She was following a course of conversation that she had rehearsed in private for a week now. "It's terrible to think that the same thing happened to her as to her father, your father in fact. Their both committing suicide, I mean."

Keith turned and looked angrily at her. "That's none of your business. In addition, my father didn't commit suicide, he had an accident."

"I don't believe that to be true and I have my reasons."

Keith was getting furious. "I'm not interested in your reasons. Go away."

"Mr Symons. You and I both know that experienced shots like your father, in good health and in their fifties, simply don't have shooting accidents. Only a fool would believe otherwise."

"My father did not commit suicide."

By now, a small circle of beaters, those who had not yet left for the pub, had formed around them at a respectful distance. They were silent and following every word of the conversation.

"Mr Symons, I know more about the circumstances of your father's death than you would like me to know. I may quite possibly know more than you do yourself. You need to find out just how much I do know."

Keith looked up. "Go ahead then. Tell me what you know, or think you know. Make it quick. I have to go."

"You are aware, of course, of the relationship which your father had with Margaret Downie in the last years before his death?"

She was getting his attention now. "Continue."

"I am referring to more than just a physical relationship. They were involved in more than that, weren't they?"

Keith blanched visibly. "I don't know what you mean."

"I think that you know all too well. They were running a call girl operation. But then they quarrelled. She threatened to reveal everything to the police. He paid her money to keep her quiet. Thirty thousand pounds in all. You know all this, don't you?"

"I most certainly don't."

"Then how come you made the last payment yourself? Of twelve thousand pounds?"

Keith was stunned. Where had she found all this out? Who was she, anyway? She clearly knew what she was talking about. "You had better watch out, Miss Brown, or I'll sue you for defamation." He took a threatening step towards Jill, who didn't move.

Whispers were being exchanged amongst the beaters. One or two heads were nodding with approval and an unspoken admiration for Jill was coming to the fore.

But there was more to come. "Will you admit that it was because your father was so shaken by the potential scandal that he committed suicide?"

Keith remained speechless. He was weakening visibly.

"And that you found a note from him that morning in the estate office in which he made clear his intention to commit suicide?

"And so?"

"And that you deliberately did not tell your mother about it?"

"What are you suggesting?"

"Go for the jugular, Jill," she said to herself. "Hit him hard!"

"I am suggesting that you deliberately destroyed the note and that you chose not to go out to shoot with your father after lunch because you knew from the note that he intended to commit suicide. You decided not to prevent him from taking his own life. You preferred to let him die by his own hand. That way the family's so-called honour would be saved, and you could get the estate. And furthermore, I am saying that you lied to your own mother, and to the police, about it all."

Keith blew up, and losing his self-control, betrayed himself. "You bitch! How did you find all this out?" He swung his gun up at her, his right hand reaching towards the trigger.

Jill felt no fear. She didn't flinch. Although she couldn't be sure, Keith had almost certainly unloaded his gun. She looked him in the eye. "Don't do anything foolish, Mr Symons."

The beaters who were watching from nearby froze and drew in their breath. Keith stood there in impotent fury, his face flushed and his hands shaking. He slowly lowered his gun, turned away and walked back in silence towards the big house.

45

John sits down heavily on the log under the alder bushes. It is the same log that he sat on about a month before with his brother Duncan. He stares out over the river. There are fresh moose tracks along the beach in front of him, but he shows no interest. Mindlessly, he starts to file his axe, first on one side of the blade then on the other. It's almost too much for him to bear, Duncan dead and then Jessica, all in the short span of three weeks. He can think of little else.

He wishes he could somehow bring his brother back to life. Despite all those years of separation, they were starting to feel close, to enjoy each other's company, as brothers should. "If only he was here with me now! We could go up into the back country together and visit the falls above the second steady. We could go out to one of the islands to look at the sea birds."

He rises slowly and goes up the trail to where it is blocked by a recent deadfall. It is a tall spruce. He severs it with a succession of heavy blows from his axe and drags the top of the tree off the trail. The intoxicating smell of fresh spruce gum fills the air. A bit hot and out of breath, he finds a nearby spot to sit down. "If Duncan hadn't had that stupid accident,

he would be out on the *Sunset Sea* by now, with Bill and Jim."
He quietly swears, removes his work gloves, and buries his
face in his hands, rubbing his hair where it is itching from his
sweat, and rubbing his eyes.

"Goddam it. Poor Duncan. Dead! It's awful. Just awful."

He gets up again and with a series of savage blows cuts the
branches off a twelve-foot length of the spruce tree. He then
makes two heavy logs and, throwing one onto each shoulder,
staggers back down the trail to the boat and drops them onto
the beach. He feels a bit better now.

"Melba will be waiting lunch for me," he thinks. However,
he doesn't want to go back yet and in any event, he's not
hungry. He returns to his seat under the alders.

He hasn't said much about Jessica to Melba, and she has
been very understanding, not asking questions, just letting
John come out with the full story of his trip in his own time.
Even so, Melba senses that Jessica was important to John,
and that her death troubles him immensely.

John closes his eyes and drops his face onto his hands.
In his own way - he is not religious - he is saying a prayer for
Jessica, just by thinking hard about her and by remembering
how she looked. He does it for a short while. It's curious what
particular image of her comes to him: not Jess in tears, nor
Jess pleading with him or suggesting to him that they go off
for a secret weekend together. Rather, it is one of Jess standing
there telling him how unhappy she is, how she considers her
life a failure.

John listens to the rumour of the river. He wishes he could
have a second chance. He would let her talk to him for as long
as necessary. He would take her into his arms and comfort
her, patiently and with compassion. Wait it out, let her get it
all out of her system. He is sure he could have succeeded in
saving her life that way. "It's too late now," he thinks. "That's
all it would have taken. I didn't have to do anything more.
I didn't have to start up our old relationship again. If I had

simply shown more sympathy and understanding, she would have accepted the rest, and she would still be alive."

He stands up and looks out across the river. "I'm sorry, Jess," he says, as the tears start to pour down his cheeks. "I'm sorry. Please forgive me."

In front of him the surface of the river is grazed by a short burst of wind, a cat's paw, that rushes towards him, briefly brushes against his face and then buries itself with a rustle into the alders behind. Once more, the river is smooth and flows implacably by, a shimmering silver mirror of the sky above.

I would like to thank Stewart Learning of Cartwright and Paradise River for the wonderful times we have had canoeing and fishing together in Central Labrador. My diaries of these trips have provided me both with an incentive, and also with some of the material with which to write The Big River.

Thanks to Paul Abraham for his wonderful illustrations, so faithful to what I have seen only in my mind's eye.

I would also like to thank my friend Meg Graham for having read the manuscript and given me the benefit of her suggestions.

Finally, I would like to thank Aaxel Author Services for their editorial and technical support, which I found outstanding.